SHOWDOWN TRAIL

Center Point
Large Print

Also by William Colt MacDonald and available from Center Point Large Print:

Gunsight Range
Lightning Swift
Ghost-Town Gold
Peaceful Jenkins
Mascarada Pass

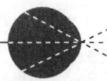

This Large Print Book carries the Seal of Approval of N.A.V.H.

SHOWDOWN TRAIL

The Red Rider of Smoky Range

William Colt MacDonald

CENTER POINT LARGE PRINT
THORNDIKE, MAINE

This Center Point Large Print edition
is published in the year 2022 by arrangement with
Golden West Inc.

Originally published in the US by Pyramid.

The text of this Large Print edition is unabridged.
In other aspects, this book may vary
from the original edition.
Printed in the United States of America
on permanent paper sourced using
environmentally responsible foresting methods.
Set in 16-point Times New Roman type.

ISBN: 978-1-63808-291-0 (hardcover)
ISBN: 978-1-63808-295-8 (paperback)

The Library of Congress has cataloged this record
under Library of Congress Control Number: 2021952483

CHAPTER 1

There were six outfits working Smoky Range that spring, the biggest of which was John Deming's Rocking-D spread. The others, still taking them according to size, were the 90-Bar, Circle-T, Broken Wheel, Rafter-H and the K-Reverse-K. Due to the late arrival of warm weather and unseasonal "northers," the calf round-up had commenced later than usual, and now every man was working with feverish haste to get the branding operations completed and head back to his home ranch.

Around three thousand cattle remained to be worked and were being held in a narrow valley which was formed by two long spurs of precipitous granite jutting eastward from the jagged peaks of the Trozar Mountain Range. It made an ideal location for holding the herd: the western limit of the valley ended abruptly against a sheer wall of rock, as did the two sides. To the east was the only outlet, and here were built the fires where the calves were branded before being pushed out to the open, grassy range beyond.

To the inexperienced eye the scene presented was one of apparent chaos. From the milling herd, shuffling with much clacking of horns in aimless circles, rumbled bellowings and bleating of calves rose through the thick clouds of dust that spread and hung in a heavy haze in the hot oppressive air. Cowboys darted here and there, swinging wide loops, or dragging helpless calves to the branding fires. Cows, infuriated at the indignities offered their offspring, charged madly, only to be caught or turned back by nimble-hoofed cow ponies.

Out of the confusion of the milling herd rode a slim young puncher, dragging at the end of his rope a struggling calf which he delivered at one of the branding fires.

Two cowhands pounced upon the unfortunate calf. One of them seized the loose skin on one side of the bleating animal, lifted it with a quick jerking movement and threw it prone. Then, holding firmly its ears, he stretched its head to one side and sat down upon it to hold it quiet. The second man cast free the lariat, then laid both hands on one of the calf's hind legs, which he pulled back as far as it would go, while the other hind leg was shoved forward by the puncher's booted foot. A brand man jerked a red-hot iron from the glowing embers of the nearest fire . . . stamped it firmly into the calf's hide.

Even before the brand-iron had been thrust back into the fire, a fourth puncher, equipped with a sharp knife, dropped down at the calf's side, accomplished certain work, then moved up to its head, where small triangles of flesh were slashed from the underside of the calf's ears.

All of this work was accomplished with such swift efficiency that the small animal had been shunted off to rejoin its mother before it realized just what had happened. The brand man grinned up at the young cowboy who had delivered the calf. "Well, well, you got another, didn't you, Jeff?"

Jeff Deming checked his horse, looked down, cold-eyed, at the speaker and nodded.

The brand man noted his attitude, hurried to continue: "You'll be a credit to your dad and the Rocking-D yet, if you keep on."

John Deming's son nodded again and said bleakly and with some sarcasm, "I wouldn't be surprised. Keeping up better than you thought for, eh?"

The brand man grinned. "Don't you worry, kid. You're doin' fine. And don't let any of these dumb rannies hooray you too much just because you got an education. Envy, I calls it. You'll show 'em a thing or two."

The hard lines faded out of Jeff Deming's features. He said, "Thanks, Buck. It takes a lot to worry me—"

The words were cut short by the arrival of three punchers, rope-dragging calves to the burning. Young Deming backed his pony out of the way.

"90-Bar," called the first puncher. "Burn the left flank. Swallow-fork the right ear!"

"Broken Wheel," announced the second man. "Right ribs! Gotch the left—"

"Rocking-D!" cut in the third rider.

John Deming's brand and ear-markings were too well-known on the Smoky Range to require further elucidation. The tally man made three swift marks with his pencil, droning meanwhile a check on the arrivals: "90-Bar—Broken Wheel—Rocking-D."

Jeff Deming reined his horse away from the fires, slowly coiling his rope, and started for the cavvy for a change of horses. His present mount was streaked with sweat and alkali dust. There was little to see of Jeff's face above the bandanna tied across his nose to prevent the entrance of dust and dirt, but his eyes were good, and his lithe young form swayed gracefully in the saddle as he rode.

"That's the trouble, all right," Jeff muttered angrily, as he peeled off his buckskin gloves and commenced to roll a cigarette. "They're all ready to jump me, because I've got some school learnin'. I realize I'm soft—out of condition—just as well as they do. But I'm doin' my share. Yes, and a heap more."

This was Jeff's first round-up in four years and the work was exhausting. Four years' absence from any line of endeavor will slow a man up. But Jeff was managing to keep up his end. He didn't object to the "kidding" that greeted him on all sides—excepting that from two or three men who had proved unusually sarcastic—whenever occasion presented. In this respect his father's foreman had proved to be the worst of the lot. For that matter, Jeff had to admit he didn't like the foreman, Quinn Barker by name. However, the elder Deming swore by Barker as a "dang good man with cows." That much practically everyone acknowledged. At the same time John Deming was inclined to underrate his son's ability, and had considered Jeff's college education a pure waste of years and effort.

Jeff scowled as his pony picked its way to the cavvy that was held by ropes tied to the chuck wagons. "Maybe I'm wrong about most of the boys resenting my college learning," he conceded finally. "I reckon they just like to hooray a feller whenever they get a chance. But, shucks, I ain't tried to lord it over 'em any. I ain't different than I ever was. Not that I know of."

Unconsciously, since returning to the range country, Jeff had reverted to the use of range idiom. His musings continued, "But there's a couple of those hombres ridin' to a sudden fall. I sure hope I don't have to cross guns with 'em, but if Quinn Barker and Trigger Texas insist on cravin' for gun-talk, I don't figure to back down any more."

He was still frowning when he reached the horses. Drawing his own pony to a halt, he swung down from the saddle, holding one hand to holster to prevent his Colt forty-five from slipping out during the movement. As his booted feet struck the dusty earth, Jeff removed his roll-brim sombrero, and with the bandanna across his nose commenced to mop his perspiration-streaked features. That done, he stuffed the bandanna in one pocket and again placed his unfinished cigarette between his lips.

At that moment a Rocking-D hand, Hefty Wilkins, now doing duty as a horse-wrangler, rounded a corner of the nearest chuck wagon. Hefty was a solidly built individual with innocent blue eyes, a good-natured countenance and straw-colored hair. The usual range togs of denim and woolen shirt covered his muscular body. "What's up, Jeff?" Hefty inquired. "Needin' a new bronc?"

Jeff nodded. "Yes. That hoss ain't tuckered so bad, but I don't figure to overwork him. He's one sweet little cuttin' pony."

"He is that," Hefty agreed, "but there's two-three others just as good. You sit down here, in the shade of this wagon, and catch a breath or two. I'll snake a fresh hoss out of your string—"

"Look here, Hefty," Jeff protested, his face flushing, "there ain't any call for you to do that. I can get my own ponies. I'm askin' favours from no one. What in hell would I be sittin' down for?"

Hefty Wilkins grinned cheerfully. "Don't you

get peeved, cow-poke. I know what you're up against. The fellers are all lookin' for you to quit cold. Wouldn't blame you much if you did. To tell the truth you're entitled to a rest. You take a man that ain't done any ridin' for four years— well, you can't expect him to have the condition for this rope and ridin' business. She's a tough game, rannie, and a four year lay-off ain't any help in standin' the gaff."

Jeff's eyes blazed. "Keepin' up my end, ain't I?" he snapped.

"You certain are," Hefty admitted. "Me, I'm admirin' your nerve a heap. You're takin' a lot of punishment, but you're takin' it like a man. Cripes! I know how you feel. There ain't a muscle in your make-up that ain't torturin' you like a toothache. You're so blame weary you can't hardly stand up, right this minute, and your sit-spot is too sore, almost, to sit down—"

"Maybe that's why I ain't takin' any rest," Jeff growled.

"That," Hefty grinned, "is plumb understandable. Shucks! Jeff, you can't hide the fact that you're plenty wore down. All the boys been watchin' you for the past several days and they're for you—strong!"

Jeff relaxed a trifle. "That's mighty agreeable to hear," he smiled. "Howsomever, I've seen some evidence to the contrary."

"Not much," Hefty stoutly defended his

declaration. " 'Course, I'll admit there's one or two that—" He broke off without finishing the words.

"I reckon," Jeff nodded, and waited for more.

Hefty opened his hands in a gesture of helplessness. "You know how it is, Jeff. A feller don't like to throw mud at a man he's workin' under, even though—"

"Loyalty is a fine virtue, Hefty," Jeff said thoughtfully. "It ain't necessary that you should say more. I know who you're referrin' to, in general. In particular, I'll add one name—Quinn Barker. Am I right?"

Hefty threw off all pretence. "Yo're right—in particular," he said frankly. "Good cowman or not, I can't see why your dad keeps Barker on his payroll. If *you* were running the Rocking-D, Barker wouldn't last five minutes, I'm bettin' a stock of hoptoads."

Jeff said slowly, "Hefty, Dad and I are a heap different. He only sees that Barker gets results with the cattle. Another thing, he never has been the same since my brother Bob was shot. Bob always was his favorite. To have Bob killed in a barroom brawl—well, Dad never said much, but I know it nearly broke his heart. He turned bitter. That, coming on top of mother's death— oh, shucks, Hefty, you know how a run of bad luck will warp a man's better judgment and turn him hard."

Hefty nodded. "I know." He paused and continued after a moment. "Jeff, did you ever hear that yore brother wa'n't killed in a fair fight—but was murdered?"

Jeff stiffened, eyes narrowing. "What you hintin' at?"

"Just what I said. I can't give you any proof, but there were rumors around—"

"I never heard anythin' of the kind—"

"You weren't here. It happened right after you went east to school, four years back. You returned long enough for the funeral, but you weren't around long enough to hear things—"

"You know anythin' definite?" Jeff cut in sharply.

"Not a thing. Sometime when we get more time—"

"You're right," Jeff nodded thoughtfully. "Maybe it will bear looking into. I've always felt sort of queer about that business myself. Bob wasn't the sort of duffer to brawl around—we'll talk it over again, Hefty. I've got to get workin'—school learnin' or no school learnin', or I'll get Barker to ridin' me."

"Surprise to me," Hefty said, "that your dad ever let you go east to college."

"Mother's doings," Jeff explained. "She made Dad promise before she died that he'd educate me . . . As for Quinn Barker—well, he's sort of afraid that I'll get the job roddin' the Rocking-D.

That's what worries him. But I won't. Barker shouldn't have any fears on that score. I won't have any more to say than any of the other hands on the payroll. Oh, Dad likes me, in his cold way, but he always did maintain that no man gets real hoss sense until he's thirty. That gives me seven years yet." Abruptly he turned away, adding, "I've got to get busy. There's no rest for the wicked."

Jeff swung around to unsaddle his weary pony. Hefty, with a quick movement, slipped behind the cowboy and with a quick jerk unbuckled the belt supporting Jeff's batwing *chaparejos* and let them sag about their owner's overall-covered knees.

Hefty laughed as Jeff grabbed for the chaps. "Now while you're pullin' up them leather pants," Hefty grinned, "I'll be saddlin' up a fresh pony for you. I had to have some sort of excuse to make you rest a few seconds."

By the time Jeff had his belt retightened, Hefty had stripped saddle and saddle blanket from the pony's back and turned it into the rope corral. With a long sigh of relief Jeff dropped to the earth with his back against a wagon wheel. It was mighty good to relax, if only for a minute. . . .

He rose as Hefty finished tightening the cinch on a fresh horse. "Much obliged, Hefty," drawing on his buckskin gloves, as the wrangler led up the new mount. "I won't be forgettin' I got one good friend in this billy-be-damned range."

"One friend hell!" Hefty exploded. "You got loads of 'em. The boys are for you. 'Course, you got to expect a mite of joshin' now and then. Trouble is, you got to thinkin' you didn't belong and you sort of drew into your shell. Hell's bells! You belong just like you always did. Right now you're a better hand than nine-tenths of the fellers on Smoky Range. Me, I been notin' how often these rannies change broncs, and you shore been changin' plenty. And your broncs is bushed when you bring 'em in, showin' they been worked hard. I ain't no fool, cowpoke. Horses don't get bushed when their riders is loafin'."

Hefty's color mounted as he warmed to his subject: "Hell, there's a heap I can see that's lot worse then you. F'rinstance, that waddy that's reppin' from the Tin-Cup outfit from over east of the Arribas Range. He won't never die from overwork. And look at that Trigger Texas hombre. Just a bum. He works hard enough when he works, but that ain't often. If Quinn Barker hadn't hired him, he wouldn't be allowed to throw a rope on this range, I'm bettin'. And Barker himself ain't so much—just average. Yeah, there's a heap of these cow-nurses that would hate to work shoulder to shoulder with you and make the showin' you've made. Yore dad will have to see that, right soon, too."

Jeff laughed ruefully. "If he sees anythin' I

15

do, I don't know it," he replied. "Dad don't pay any more attention to me than he would to some stranger reppin' from a distant range."

"I know, I know," Hefty nodded quickly. He removed a battered sombrero and ran puzzled fingers through his bushy hair. Then gave some pertinent advice: "You'll just have to make him notice you, Jeff. Snap back at a few of these mouthy hombres that have been ridin' you. Frankly, some of the fellers been wonderin' when you'd start showin' a mite of spirit—"

"I'll show 'em plenty," Jeff stated grimly, "if that's all they want." He put one foot in stirrup and swung up to the pony's back, settled himself in saddle. Then he looked down into Hefty's concerned features. "It's this way, Hefty; ever since I came home I been keepin' my mouth shut. I figured the boys might think my head had grown bigger than natural if I talked too much. I've held myself from talkin' purposely, so they wouldn't get an idea I was tryin' to show off. I reckon I leaned too far in the wrong direction."

"That's it, exactly," Hefty nodded vehement agreement. "Now, you lean a mite in the other direction—and lean *hard* against these hombres that have been runnin' off at the head so promiscuous like."

"Meanin'," Jeff smiled gravely, "Quinn Barker? All right, I'll be ready for Barker—"

"Don't you go forgettin'," Hefty warned

16

earnestly, "that Barker is afflicted with an itchy trigger finger."

Jeff's features tightened into grim lines. "I'm forgettin' nothin', cowboy. There's one thing I did do while I was away at school: I had my gun with me and I used to get out in the country, every chance, and practice my shootin'. I haven't lost any speed in the last four years, Hefty. No, I'm not forgettin'—and I'm not worryin' either about Barker's rep as a lead-slinger. If he's itchin' for trouble, it's li'ble to happen to him!"

CHAPTER 2

Three men had arrived at the branding fires almost simultaneously with their captured calves. The three were John Deming, owner of the Rocking-D; Quinn Barker, his foreman; and Trigger Texas, one of the Rocking-D hands.

Except that his face was a trifle more lined, John Deming's features were the counterpart of Jeff's. There were the same slate-grey eyes, straight nose, black hair and determined mouth and chin. Like his son, there wasn't an ounce of superfluous flesh on the man's lean frame, and he sat his horse with the lightness of a youngster. John Deming had never been the man to stand idly by and watch other men do all the work. This attitude, doubtless, accounted for his perfect condition and active bearing.

Quinn Barker, too, was well-built. He was in his early thirties. A small black moustache adorned his upper lip and he possessed the dark swarthy complexion of an Apache Indian, though so far as anyone *knew* there wasn't a drop of alien blood in his veins. He was attired in the customary chaps, flannel shirt and sombrero. A six-shooter swung at his right hip.

The third man of the arriving trio, Trigger Texas, was a muscular individual with a broken nose, a month's growth of beard and an angular frame. Texas was considered a bad man with a gun. He was lazy, and folks in the Smoky Range country invariably spoke of him as "that bum, Texas." He had been with the Rocking-D only a few months, and in that time most of his wages had gone for liquor. There were many who thought that Texas might have spent some of his wages for a decent pair of overalls.

His attire was tattered, battered and torn, from the peak of his ragged-brimmed sombrero to the broken spurs that adorned the rundown heels of his riding-boots. Occasionally he washed and shaved—not often. He was as hard and tough as they come in the southwest cow-country, however, and disdained the use of leather cuffs or gloves. His shirt sleeves were rolled to the elbow, revealing the heavy red underwear that covered his brawny arms. Despite his name, he wasn't a native of the Lone Star State, for which the *Tejanos* of Smoky Range were duly thankful.

John Deming had delivered his calf and was coiling his lariat, preparatory to riding back to the herd, when he caught Quinn Barker's words addressed to Trigger Texas: "Here comes young Deming. Watch me have some fun with him. I'll throw him on the prod and see if he's got the nerve of a jackrabbit, which same I doubt."

Deming checked his horse a short distance away and waited, unknown to Barker and Texas, to see how Jeff would accept the foreman's words. In a few moments Jeff came riding past from the cavvy on his way back to the herd. He noticed Barker watching him, but proceeded on his way until Barker spoke:

"Well, kid, stallin' again, eh? Figured we wouldn't spot you loafin' in the shade of that wagon, didn't you?"

Jeff laughed scornfully, wheeled his pony toward the speaker. He didn't speak until he had drawn to a halt facing Barker and Texas. Then he said quietly, "I wasn't stalling and I *did* expect *you* to see me. You seem to have a habit of seeing things that aren't any of your business."

Barker stiffened with surprise. The reply was unexpected. Usually when spoken to in this manner, it had been Jeff's custom to nod and ride on, face flushing crimson, without replying. Now the young cowboy's features were set in a calm, determined mask, his lips straight and firm, grey eyes narrowed to thin slits that would have spelled trouble to a more cautious man than Barker was proving himself to be.

Those within earshot halted activities to listen. The men at the branding fires looked up in sudden approval. Two or three nodded with satisfaction upon noting Jeff's defiant attitude. What the elder Deming's opinions were, no man could say. The owner of the Rocking-D sat his horse, watching the scene, his face immobile.

Quinn Barker recovered from his surprise, commenced to laugh it off. "Cripes!" he commented sarcastically, "you needn't get riled at us poor uncouth cowmen, just because you went to college to learn how to raise beef animals. We do the best we can. 'Course, we admit we ain't high-toned educated like you, but—"

"That's enough of that, too," Jeff snapped, backing his horse a step. "From now on, Barker, you can treat me like any of the rest of the men. I'm not askin' for any more—and I'll be takin' no less. That applies not only to you, but to anyone else that feels called upon to ride me. Can you understand that? I've had just about enough of your nasty talk. Is that clear?"

Barker's face flamed. "I get you," he rasped. "In other words, you're lookin' for trouble. All right, you'll get it. On account of your paw, I been nursin' you along."

"I'm askin' to be treated like the other men," Jeff repeated, cutting in coldly on Barker's words, "and said treatment doesn't consist of any more sneering remarks from you. I've had enough of that sort of thing."

"By Gawd!" Barker snarled, "I will treat you like the other Rocking-D hands. Next time I catch you loafin', you can get your roll and drift. You'll be fired, see?"

"There's likely to be a heap of firin' goin' on if that's all it takes," Jeff retorted meaningly. "I'm not referrin' to any of the other brands, but it might be a good idea to check into some of the hombres *you've* hired on this range. They don't need to be so careful of their throw ropes. Ropes don't break easy—"

Trigger Texas cut in nastily, "You wouldn't be mentionin' any names in particular, would you, kid? Me, fr'instance?"

Jeff flashed a quick glance at Texas. "It goes as it lays," he said frigidly. "I'm throwin' a community loop that's meant to circle any hombre that ain't got the kinks worked out of his hemp yet. If you get caught in that circle, Texas, you know who I'm referrin' to. If you don't like my *habla*, it's your next move. I've dealt my cards. Now, it's up to you to play your hand or get out of the game."

Texas cursed and jerked his horse around to face Jeff's right, but before he could make any sort of reply to Jeff's challenge, John Deming spurred his pony in between the two. "C'mon, men," he ordered shortly. "I won't have any wrangling when there's work to be done. Jeff, you get busy cuttin', Barker, you and Texas get back to the herd. You're paid to handle stock— not waste the time I pay wages for. Now, start ridin'—*pronto!*"

Without waiting for an answer, the elder Deming wheeled his horse and in a few moments was lost in the clouds of dust that welled up from the vicinity of the cattle herd. Jeff bit his lip, glanced contemptuously at Barker and Texas, then started toward the milling cows. Texas and Barker rode slowly away from the branding fires, talking in low tones, and followed by the glances of the brand men. No doubt about it, Jeff's new attitude had raised him in the estimation of all within hearing.

By this time, Jeff's horse had carried him nearer to the herd. Touching spurs to his pony's sides he dashed in among the cattle. Once more the alkali commenced to bite eyes and throat and nostrils, but Jeff held grimly to his task as he guided the horse through the crush of moving cattle. All around him was a vast sea of tossing horns.

Down at the heels of the herd, half hidden by dust, he spied a small red calf, twisting and dodging close to its mother. Jeff spoke to his horse, plunged in, and commenced to drive the cow toward the flank of the densely packed herd. Twice the cow turned and tried to dodge back, and twice the wise little cow-pony, sensing the movements before they came, headed her off, nipping the animal's hide in a manner that sent her scurrying to the rim of the herd, followed by her calf.

By the time they had cleared the crush of milling animals, Jeff had shaken out his loop and raised his hand for the cast. Even as he whirled it through the air, he saw, from the corner of his eye, Trigger Texas and Quinn Barker but a short distance away. Settling down to business, Jeff released the rope. The hempen noose went sailing swiftly through the air . . . settled about the rear right leg of the calf. . . .

At the same instant, a second rope flashed out of the dust haze at one side and struck Jeff cruelly across the face! For a moment he was blinded by the unexpected attack . . . thrown off balance. His body jerked back, his spurs raking the little cow-pony. The horse snorted, jumped madly to one side and, already unsettled, Jeff went sprawling from its back. Even as he struck the earth, his ears caught the jeering laughter of Barker and Texas.

Jeff scrambled angrily to his feet and not a moment too soon. The cow, resenting the indignity put upon her calf, came plunging, head down, toward the cowboy. Jeff stooped swiftly, then straightened up. Just as the cruel horns were almost upon him, he side-stepped and hurled a double handful of dust into the cow's eyes. The animal stopped abruptly, sliding to haunches, then wheeled, angrily shaking her head and bellowing. The next instant, Jeff had regained his pony's side and vaulted into the saddle.

"Good hoss," Jeff muttered through his heat. The pony had held taut the rope running from saddlehorn to the calf. The little bovine was just straggling to its feet when the cowboy jerked his mount around and started for the fire, dragging the squirming calf at his rear. By this time, Trigger Texas had herded the blinded cow to one side. All the fight had been taken from the animal by this time.

From behind came a series of sarcastic remarks as Jeff rode toward the branding fire. Barker and Texas thought that Jeff was going to let the incident pass unmentioned and for a few moments they allowed themselves a fit of hearty laughter.

But by this time, Jeff was "seeing red." He delivered the calf at the fire, jerked out,

"K-Reverse-K on the left shoulder! Underslope right and left."

The tally man echoed the words, Jeff's rope was released and, coiling it as he moved, he headed directly back toward the herd, his grey eyes burning with a cold flame of righteous anger.

Chape Stock, the grizzled old owner of the K-Reverse-K, who was handling an iron at the fire straightened his aching back and looked seriously after Jeff, a look of concern in his weather-beaten features.

One of the men holding the prone calf urged, "Better hurry it, Chape. This is one of your own critters. Yore iron's gettin' cold."

Stock nodded, wiped sweat from his forehead

and applied the branding iron. Smoke curled up in his face. He removed his iron, commenting shortly, "Looks to me as if young Deming might be aimin' to heat an iron—"

"Huh?" from a knife man.

"Shootin' iron, I'm talkin' about," Chape Stock grunted. "That boy shore had blood in his eyes when he left here. Wonder if he's had more trouble with Barker or Texas. He talked plenty turkey to that pair a spell back, you'll remember. Mebbe they've took up the gauntlet—"

By this time, Jeff was nearing the spot at which Texas and Barker were sitting their ponies side by side. Cows and cowhands moved all around them while the pair talked in low tones. They pretended not to see Jeff's approach. When Jeff had come within a few yards of the pair he drew rein and looked steadily at Barker without speaking.

Barker looked up, caught that steady gaze for a moment, then looked away.

Jeff said, "Barker."

Barker's eyes flamed with hate as he said, "Well?"

"It's not well at all," Jeff replied in cold tones. "I'm askin' for an explanation."

Barker looked from side to side, then back at Jeff. Reluctantly he muttered, "Sorry that happened, Jeff. It just worked out that we was throwin' at the same calf. I didn't see you—"

"Either you're a rotten hand with a rope," Jeff declared, "or your throw was intentional. I'm thinkin' it was the last. If so, that stunt was the work of a skunk."

Barker's face crimsoned, then went white with rage. For a moment he couldn't speak. In the confusion of the round-up work, no one noticed the three men, except one cowboy who had pulled to a halt, to watch proceedings, some short distance away.

Trigger Texas took up the conversation: "It was yore own fault, kid. You shouldn't have tried to rope a dogie that we was after—"

"We?" Jeff said scornfully. "Does it take two of you to cut one animal?"

"That was it," Barker cut in, "you was loafin' again. Why in hell don't you cut out yore own animals? That cow was plumb unruly and showin' fight. Me'n Texas had been workin' on her. Here we went to all the work of separatin' the damn critter from her calf and then you wait on the outside of the herd to rope the dogie. If my rope hit you in the face, it's yore own fault the accident happened. You should have kept out of my way."

The bald-faced nerve of the pair almost took Jeff's breath away. When he finally replied, his tones were like chilled steel, "I cut those animals and you both know it. If you, Barker, figured to dab your string on that calf, you were sure throwin' plumb high, that's all. Either that or you don't know the first thing about handlin' a rope. Which was it?"

"Look here," Barker snarled, "are you insinuatin' that—"

"Nope, I'm not insinuatin'," Jeff snapped. "I'm statin' facts—fiat out. I'm wishin' there was a stamp iron in that fire yonderly, bearin' the word 'liar' on it. I'd be plumb tempted to hogtie both of you and brand you with the mark you ought to be wearin'. Seein' there ain't no such iron, I'm tellin' you to your faces—you're as fine a pair of damned liars as I ever encountered!"

This was war talk with a vengeance. Texas swiftly spurred to one side, right hand hovering close to the six-shooter at his hip. Jeff met the maneuver by quickly shifting his own position so as to watch both men. One hand gripped his pony's reins; the thumb of the other hand was hooked in cartridge belt.

No one spoke for a moment. Cattle milled around throwing a grey haze about the three men. Barker opened his mouth to speak, then changed his mind. He and Texas glared at the young cowboy. Texas finally laughed coldly and prompted his foreman, "He's askin' for it, Quinn."

Jeff didn't move. He said mockingly, "Had to tell him, didn't you, Texas?"

Barker swore at him in a hoarse strained voice,

adding, "Them's fightin' words, Deming. I reckon you might just as well have it now as any time." His hand dropped to gun-butt.

Still Jeff made no move. There was a world of cold scorn in his voice now: "Certainly they're fightin' words. Have you got enough nerve to see it through?"

Barker's gun-barrel flashed out . . . up . . . belched flame and smoke. But his draw had come a fraction of a second too late. Jeff's Colt gun had seemed to leap to meet his eager fingers. A lance-like tongue of white fire darted from the muzzle!

Quinn Barker clapped one hand to his breast, dropped his gun and swayed in the saddle. Quite suddenly he toppled to the ground.

Jeff whirled to meet Trigger Texas, whose gun was already out. At that instant the roar of a forty-five thundered through the din of the round-up. Before Texas could fire, a streak of crimson had appeared as though by magic across the back of his gun-hand; the weapon slipped from his grasp.

There came a sudden pounding of hoofs as a lean, young, red-haired puncher swept up in a whirl of dust and gravel, six-shooter gripped in his right hand, and pulled to a long, sliding halt.

Jeff turned to the newcomer, "Much obliged, Three-Star," he said tersely. "You probably saved my life." He cast an angry look at the disgruntled Texas, who was nursing a wounded hand.

"Cripes," Texas growled, "I wa'n't aimin' to throw down on you, Jeff. I figured mebbe you'd be gunnin' for me and I was just aimin' to pertect myself—"

"You're a liar, Texas," snapped the Rocking-D puncher known as Three-Star Hennessey. His blue eyes flashed indignantly, sending waves of crimson anger up into the roots of his rebellious thatch of sorrel-colored hair. "You're a liar. I been watching you. I saw what happened. Barker went for his gun first. You were ready to follow up if necessary. You were both out to down Jeff. If I was Jeff I'd blast you from hell to breakfast—"

Other men were riding up now. Excited questions and answers flew back and forth.

Hennessey was smiling grimly as he replied to the words of one of the cowhands, "Good shootin' nothin', rannie. I ain't that good. My pony was movin' too fast for good shootin'. All I thought of was pluggin' Texas where he'd be stopped fast before he could throw down on Jeff. It was just sheer luck for him that my slug grazed his hand. I was aimin' at his body. . . ."

John Deming came loping up, his face clouded with anger, and demanded to know what happened. Jeff told the story briefly while some of the hands worked over the unconscious Barker. Jeff realized, from his father's expression, when the story was concluded, that John Deming held his son to blame for the fight.

"Look here, Jeff," the elder Deming snapped. "Quinn Barker has worked for me long enough for me to know him pretty well. You're evading something. Quinn wouldn't deliberately hit you in the face with his rope. It was an accident, clearly enough. You employed the incident to make trouble. You're too hot-headed—"

"That's just the way we was tryin' to explain it," Trigger Texas cut in eagerly. "Quinn had apologized like a gent. We figured the business was finished when all of a sudden Jeff loses his temper, jerks his gun and started shootin'." While Texas talked, he employed one hand to bind a filthy bandanna around his wounded fingers. "It was all an accident. Quinn and Jeff was both throwin' at the same calf. They'd made a mistake as to who it belonged to—"

"Cut it, Texas," Jeff interrupted. "There wasn't any mistake about it when we were arguing the matter. At that time you were *sure* it was yours and Barker's. Have you forgotten your claim that you and Barker cut it out together? I'm the hombre that's supposed to be loafin' but I manage to cut my cows without any help—"

"Keep quiet, Jeff," John Deming ordered sternly. "Let Texas tell his story."

"Well, that's the how of it," Texas insisted, not meeting Jeff's eyes. "Then Jeff and Quinn had some words and, sudden, Jeff jerked his hawglaig and commenced shootin'. Poor Quinn, he was so took by surprise that he never had a chance—"

"That's a lie," Three-Star Hennessey cut in heatedly. "I saw that part of the fracas. Barker pulled first. Jeff beat him to the shot. I don't know where Barker's slug went. Next Texas drew his gun to get into the mix-up and—well, I stopped that play."

"And I'll be gettin' you for that, first chance—" Texas commenced, snarling.

"Start now, if yore feelin' thataway," Three-Star invited belligerently. "I've heard you boast you could shoot as well with one hand as t'other—"

"Stop it!" John Deming barked. "You men stop these arguments and get back to work. This round-up has got to be finished plenty pronto, and we can't afford to be delayed by fighting. Jeff, I'll be holding your gun and Texas's and Three-Star's, until you've all had time to cool down. Hand 'em over, you three."

As round-up boss, John Deming had a perfect right to demand this and the men knew it. The guns were surrendered without a protest.

The elder Deming, followed by Jeff and Three-Star, made his way to the blanket upon which Barker was stretched.

"Quinn hurt serious?" Deming snapped.

One of the men kneeling on the ground at Barker's side looked up. "It don't look encouragin'," he admitted, "but I reckon with proper care he could pull through. Jeff's slug struck too high to be downright dangerous. If we had a doctor we might—"

"We'll get him to town," Deming stated quickly, "where he can be under a doctor's care. No use bringin' a doctor 'way out here." He turned to Jeff, "Jeff, you and Three-Star hitch up a wagon and drive into Gunsmoke City with Barker. Get him to the doctor as soon as you can, then both of you make statements to the sheriff. I'll have Texas ride in and tell his side of the story to Sheriff Eaton later. I want Eaton to hear both sides of this argument, in case Barker dies. Don't let Eaton hold either of you. I need you here. Tell him I'll be responsible for your appearance any time you're needed."

So long as John Deming held the guns of the three men he felt confident there'd be no renewal of the fight. Just to make sure, however, he didn't intend to let Texas leave the round-up camp until Jeff and Hennessey were nearly to Gunsmoke City. After giving his orders, John Deming climbed to the saddle without another word and headed back toward the herd.

Jeff and Three-Star had commenced to hitch up a team. Three-Star said flatly, "I was sure glad to see you throw down on Barker, if you want my opinion. He's been ridin' you ever since this round-up started. He had it comin'. Hefty Wilkins and me both been waitin' for you to start somethin', and Barker deserved everythin' he got."

Jeff nodded moodily. "Yeah, I reckon so. But after the work is finished, I can see myself tanglin' with Dad. He's square—square as the devil—but he makes mistakes of judgment now and then, then refuses to be shown when he's wrong. He figures I'm not old enough to have any opinions of my own. Right now, he's certain in his own mind that I'm to blame for the fight with Barker and Texas. And if Barker lives—"

"Hope he don't," Three-Star growled.

Jeff swallowed heavily. "I can't say I'd go so far as to say that," he said slowly. "I'd be willing to let the whole matter drop now, but I know Barker wouldn't have it that way. That will bring on a battle, and there's no tellin' what way it would turn out. I'm certain of just one thing—the Rocking-D isn't big enough to hold both of us."

"Cowboy, you worry about that when the time comes," Hennessey advised. "Barker won't bother you for quite a spell now anyway. C'mon, the team's hitched. We got a ride ahead of us."

CHAPTER 3

Quinn Barker didn't die.

Jeff hadn't been arrested for the shooting. Three-Star Hennessey's story that Jeff fired in self-defense and the fact that Jeff was John Deming's son, carried some weight in the matter of his release, despite the protestations of Trigger Texas that the fault had been wholly Jeff's. Later, John Deming questioned Barker, with the consequence that the elder Deming still felt the gun-fight was of Jeff's inception.

However, after the excitement had definitely subsided and it became certain that Barker wouldn't die, John Deming termed the subject closed and didn't mention it again to Jeff, though there was an added coolness in his attitude in all his relations with his son. Jeff, considerably embittered, had already decided to make no further advances toward his father, and thus a sort of veiled hostility existed between the two. Finally the point was reached where they rarely spoke to each other except on matters of ranch business, and any of Jeff's suggestions in this direction were abruptly disregarded. John Deming was apparently trying to make Jeff understand that, though he was the son of the owner, his opinions carried no more weight than any other of the hired hands. In short, a sort of armed neutrality existed between father and son, and Jeff had about decided to leave the Rocking-D and head for parts unknown. He realized that such a situation couldn't continue indefinitely; that eventually a flare-up must be the logical result of such circumstances.

There hadn't been any renewal of the outbreak between Trigger Texas and Hennessey. Both had returned to their work, with Barker's *segundo*, Gabe Torango, being elevated to the position of temporary foreman, and, in time, affairs were progressing as smoothly as ever—at least on the surface of appearances.

However, Jeff felt, and in this belief he was seconded by Three-Star and Hefty Wilkins, that Barker and Trigger Texas were only biding their time until an opportunity to adjust certain matters occurred. Quinn Barker was longheaded, and there wasn't the least doubt in Jeff's mind but that Texas, in his present peaceful attitude, was only acting under orders from Barker. Once the temporarily disabled foreman was back in the saddle and running things, trouble would break out in no indefinite manner, and when and how it would end no man could say. Such were the suspicions growing stronger in Jeff's mind.

It was at sundown one evening that Jeff was seated on the gallery of the big, rambling Rocking-D ranch house. The cowboy slept in the bunk-house with the other hands, but occasionally he came to sit on the spot where, for many years, his mother had loved to take her daily respite from household labors and watch the light die out of the western sky.

An evening breeze rustled the sagebrush with gentle fingers, bringing a certain fragrance to his nostrils. Back of the house a horse whinnied from a corral. Laughing voices and the strumming of a guitar reached him from the bunk-house. A lump formed in Jeff's throat, his eyes grew a trifle misty. This was nice country. He didn't like to think about leaving the Rocking-D. . . .

A footstep sounded at Jeff's rear. John Deming stepped through the doorway of the main room to the gallery. "Thought I'd find you here when you didn't come to supper," Deming said briefly.

"I'll get a snack from Cookie later," Jeff said. "I wanted to watch the sun go down."

The elder Deming sneered, "That somethin' you learned at college?"

Jeff flushed. He kept his voice steady, "Nope, I learned to do this a good many years ago. You ought to know that," he said softly. His mind was travelling back across a score of years when his mother had held him on her lap at this very spot.

John Deming's throat cleared noisily. He knew what Jeff was thinking of. There was an uncomfortable silence for a few moments. Then the elder Deming hardened his features and came abruptly to the point: "Quinn Barker will be back with us tomorrow morning. You'll take orders from him—"

Jeff rose quickly to his feet. "Not with *us,* he won't. I reckon I might as well say good-bye now."

"What's that? What do you mean?" Deming dropped into the chair vacated by his son and frowned back over one shoulder.

Jeff stood looking down at his father, face serious. He said quietly, "Simply that the Rocking-D isn't big enough to hold both of us— not without trouble. One of us is bound to go. I don't like to shoot a man unless I have to. I'm trying to avoid a repetition of what happened during spring brandin'—so I reckon I'll be driftin'."

John Deming swore in a low voice that shook with anger. Finally, "You sit down a minute, Jeff. Yo're too hot-headed. I aim to talk to you. Sit down, I said!"

Reluctantly Jeff pulled up another chair. "Shoot," he invited shortly, irritated by his father's attitude.

Deming spoke slowly, choosing his words with care. "It's like this—I saw Quinn in town today, talked things over with him. I've persuaded him to let bygones be bygones. He promised me not to hold that shootin' against you—"

"So kind of him," Jeff murmured sarcastically, "when he started the whole thing—"

"That ain't true," Deming snapped. "Quinn has told me—"

"You'd take Barker's word against mine?" Jeff's eyes burned hotly.

"In the present instance—yes. It's the word of an experienced man against that of a boy. Had Barker drawn first, you wouldn't have had a chance. I've seen Barker shoot—at targets, of course. He's good. And yet you try to tell me that after four years' absence from the handling of firearms, you could—" Deming broke off, endeavored to control his tones which had been rising higher and higher. "Look here, Jeff, I'll grant you this much. You may have thought that Barker was reaching for his gun. Yo're hot-headed, too ready to fight—"

"Then why," Jeff queried steadily, "do you care whether I stay here or not?"

"Yo're my son," John Deming stated stiffly. "My name means something in this country. I've made the Deming Rocking-D iron something to be proud of. I have the respect of all in this county. My brand is known far and wide. I'm trying to do my duty by you, raise you up to be a credit to the name of Deming. Instead"—again his voice rose—"you insist on spilling the blood of yore neighbors on the name, making a disgrace of—"

"That's enough, Dad," Jeff cut in. "I don't like lead-slingin' any better than you, but no man's going to ride me ragged and—"

"That's the point right there," Deming jerked out. "You're wearin' a chip on yore shoulder, goin' around huntin' trouble. I thought you'd be different, but yo're followin' the trail made by yore brother, Bob—just another barroom brawler with a ready gun and a savage tongue. You—"

"Just a minute!" Jeff's tones were sharp. "I never knew Bob to be a barroom brawler—"

"You know what happened. You heard the story—"

"I heard the story that Quinn Barker told you. That Bob had got drunk in the Red Tiger Saloon—a lowdown dirty dive if there ever was one—and made war talk to some professional gunman. Guns were pulled and Bob killed."

"Exactly," John Deming agreed. "What you say about the Red Tiger is true, too. It was a dirty dive. As a matter of fact, it was Barker himself who first suggested that I have the sheriff close up the place and run its owner and patrons out of town. You can't deny that."

"No," Jeff retorted, "but I'll suggest that was one way of getting rid of damaging evidence. Barker never appeared openly in that clean-up. Everybody thinks it was your doings—"

"What evidence you talking about?"

"Just a minute, Dad. Did you ever hear that

Bob was murdered—not killed in a fair fight?"

"Bosh! There were rumors to that effect, but I have Quinn Barker's word. He saw the whole thing—"

"What became of the man who shot Bob—the gunman he quarreled with?"

"He was exonerated by a coroner's jury, and later left town. He shot in self-defense. I don't know where he went. He was wounded, if you'll remember. One of Bob's shots broke his arm, but not until he had shot Bob. Yo're too—"

"Wait a minute, we're getting somewhere now," Jeff pursued steadily. "Who picked that coroner's jury?"

"Old Doc Rathbone, the man who examined Bob—"

"Exactly. Rathbone. A drunken sot if there ever was one. It didn't come out until a year later that he had no authority to practice medicine. He left town hurriedly, I understand." Jeff added, "None of the coroner's jury is in Gunsmoke City any more either. They drifted away."

"Humph!" Deming grunted sarcastically. " 'Pears like you been brushin' up on local history."

"I have," Jeff admitted quietly. "There's quite a bit of knowledge to be picked up in town if a man will only listen long enough. Three-Star and Hefty have helped too—"

"Yo're wastin' yore time," gruffly. "I never yet

saw a gun-fight, where somebody was killed, that didn't result in a whole corral of rumors and conjecturin' flyin' around. Folks hear things, repeat 'em, and the first thing you know, they're believin' 'em. What if everybody connected with that shootin' has left town—"

"Not everybody," Jeff pointed out. "Only those who might talk."

"Rats!" Deming growled. "You ain't yet told me anythin' that backs up that murder suspicion of yours."

Jeff sighed, then, "Listen, Dad, you know as well as I that Bob wasn't a heavy drinker. I know that he didn't make a habit of drinkin' at the Red Tiger. When I was a youngster he warned me, more than once, never to go there. Answer this, how did Barker happen to be in the Red Tiger?"

"He'd heard that Bob was drunk there and making gun talk. Went there to bring him home," Deming replied promptly. "As he came in the front door, he saw the two men going for guns. He was too late to stop the fight. Bob was killed." John Deming's features were set in stern, relentless lines. "It's hard to say it of my own flesh and blood, but Bob is better in his grave than—"

"Forget that a minute," Jeff said wearily. "Dad, did you ever hear that Bob had been shot in the back—"

"Rot!" Deming growled. "There were only two shots fired—Bob's and the other man's—"

"It's rumored there were three reports—the third one just as Barker entered the doorway at Bob's back—"

"Do you believe such foolishness?"

"Barker was seen to reload his gun and run a rag through the barrel a few minutes later—"

"Cripes!" impatiently. "Somebody's fillin' you full of guff. The bullet entered Bob's chest—"

"So old Doc Rathbone claimed," Jeff agreed, "but nearly a year later he got drunk one night and talked plenty—"

"What do you mean?"

"Rathbone stated that the bullet in Bob's chest was too high to kill instantly, and that it was a slug below the left shoulder blade that had brought death. The next day, when sober, Rathbone denied making any such statement, but the words weren't forgotten. Two days later, he and Barker were seen to be having hot words on the street—"

"About what?" skeptically.

"That I don't know. Nobody seems to have caught the gist of the argument, except it is stated that Barker looked worried when the two parted. Two weeks later the news got out that Rathbone wasn't legally entitled to practice his profession. And I hear he left town in a mighty great hurry."

Savagely, John Deming packed tobacco in a

brier pipe, scratched a match, puffed furiously for a few minutes. Finally he asked acidly, "It'll just take one question to blow your argument to hell, Jeff. What reason would Quinn Barker have for bringing about Bob's death? Not a reason on earth. No, I can't put any faith in such tales—"

Jeff smiled wryly. "You're stubborn, Dad. All right, here's a reason. It's rumored—"

"More rumors. Bah!"

"—that Bob came riding into town, looking for Barker. He was heard to say that he had evidence that Barker was rustling—your cattle. He carried a skinned-out section of cowhide which showed a Wagon-Wheel brand burned over the Rocking-D—"

"Now look here, Jeff," angrily, "are you hintin' that Steel's Broken Wheel outfit has been stealin' my—"

"I said Wagon-Wheel—not Broken Wheel," Jeff interrupted. "Two different brands if you'll give a minute of thought to it. Anyway, Barker was seen to ride into town a short time before Bob, but he kept out of Bob's way. It's my belief that Bob caught him red-handed and Barker managed to make a getaway. A short time later, somebody brought word to Bob that Barker was in the Red Tiger. Bob went there. Barker wasn't there, but Bob's killer was. I don't know what started the argument, but Barker came in as the two men were drawing guns. Later, Barker was seen to give Bob's killer—supposed killer, that is—a sum of money. Then the man left town."

It was dark now. John Deming puffed savagely on his brier, the red glow from the bowl throwing into bold relief the lines of his stern, unbelieving face.

"You don't believe me, do you?" Jeff said at last.

Deming grunted, without making reply. Jeff drew out a sack of Durham and commenced rolling a cigarette. His match scratched noisily in the night silence.

Finally, the elder Deming knocked the dottle out of his pipe and replied to Jeff's question. "No, I don't believe you, Jeff."

"I was afraid you wouldn't."

"Why should I?" irritatedly. "You've admitted all you've said is based on rumors. Show me proof and I'll ask Barker—"

"If I had proof," Jeff snapped, "you wouldn't get time to ask Barker anythin'. I'd handle the matter myself. I'd—"

"Pull up short there," Deming growled. "You're runnin' off at the head again. Now, I'll do the talkin'. I've give careful thought to everythin' you've said, and I know it's all a pack of lies— lies and *loco* rumors started by trouble-makers. Quinn Barker has been with me goin' on five years. He's proved that he knows cows. He gets out and works—"

"He wouldn't dare do otherwise when you do the same."

"That's neither here nor there. He's proved himself a good man for the Rocking-D. I've made money on my beef. Once or twice Barker and me have disagreed on policies, but we always talked things over quiet until one or the other was proved wrong. We've done things on that basis. Knowin' him like I do, I'd trust him from hell to breakfast. I'm a pretty good judge of men, if I do say so myself—"

"I wouldn't trust him any farther than I could throw a steer by the tail."

"Yo're young yet—ain't reached mature judgment. Now I don't want to hear no more of this murder talk. It's nonsense. I wouldn't insult Barker by even mentionin' it to him—though he's probably heard of all those rumors."

Jeff sighed hopelessly and Deming went on, "Why, the man has proved his worth by his attitude toward you. He told me today he didn't hold the fight against you. He's broad-minded—"

"Probably wants a chance to shoot me in the back," Jeff growled.

"That's enough of that," sharply. "Yo're actually lookin' for trouble, while Quinn is offerin' you the hand of friendship. Are you goin' to be bull-headed enough to refuse, or are you going to stay on the Rocking-D payroll?"

Jeff said slowly, "I might stick around just in

hope of finding proof to back up those rumors. I'll never quit lookin' for proof—"

"I refuse to listen to that sort of talk," Deming said harshly. "Yo're slanderin' an innocent man. The question is, are you goin' to work here peacefully, or are you goin' to keep up this hot-headed attitude that—"

"Just a minute, Dad." Jeff considered. He disliked to quarrel with his father. If the matter could be adjusted peacefully and without the relinquishment of any rights, Jeff was inclined to stay on in the hopes that eventually he and his father might effect a state of closer, more cordial understanding.

"It's this way, Dad," Jeff continued, "if I remain, after Barker returns, will I be taking orders from him, or will you listen to a few of my own ideas regarding the raising of beef cattle? I hate to have my education wasted—"

"Now, look here, Jeff," Deming exploded, "I don't want any of yore book-taught theories. Cattle were raised for food long before books were printed and things have to be worked out in practice before—"

"Granted, but I'm only offering what has already proved successful—"

"So the college professors say," the elder Deming sneered. "They have to have somethin' to teach or they'd lose their jobs. No. I don't want to hear any more of such talk. You ain't had

47

experience enough to have a say in the breeding of Rocking-D stock. Barker's a dang good cowman, knows his—"

"I'm willing to admit that much. At the same time, he's not too old to learn a few more tricks—"

"Book tricks ain't needed," Deming stated sourly. "I'm sick of such talk. You couldn't do no better than to work under Barker for a spell. Just because you've put in four years at an agricultural college, you got an idea you know it all. You may have certain theories, but you need practical experience."

"Dammit, Dad," Jeff said testily, "you're too stubborn to admit it, but I knew as much about ranchin' before I went east as Barker does right now."

"Provin' then," the older man laughed sarcastically, "what I've always maintained—yore goin' to school was just a waste of good time and money."

Jeff smiled in the darkness, endeavored to hold his temper. "Two years ago," he pointed out, "when Smoky Range was overrun with scab, and cows were dropping right and left, and you were all running yourselves *loco*, wonderin' what to do, I remember sendin' you a lime and sulphur formula to be employed as a dip. You never even acknowledged receiving it, but since I've been back a heap of cowmen have told me that that dip saved the situation for every stock-raiser on the range. You had Quinn Barker with you then. Why didn't he know what to do?"

Deming squirmed in his chair. Finally, when he could control his voice, he snapped, "That wa'n't nothin' that come out of yore head. You needn't to take credit for it."

"I'm not," Jeff replied earnestly, "but that's just one of the things I learned at school—provin' that my four years of study wasn't wasted. If you only stop to figure up the cash that that formula saved you stockmen, you'll realize that the cost of my schooling wasn't wasted either. Be sensible, Dad. I'm not a kid. Give me some credit. You and I can get together and—"

"Cripes A'mighty!" John Deming leaped up, losing his temper. "I've had enough of this kind of talk. Either you stay here or you don't. I don't much care which! I've tried to do my best by you so you'd be a credit to the Deming name, but I'm damned if I'll take any more back-lip from the likes of you. I've tried to be patient. I've listened to what you had to say. I've overlooked a lot, even when you've as much as told me to my face that you prefer to believe a herd of scandal-mongers in town rather than yore own father. I don't like the way you've been acting at all. I won't stand for—"

Jeff cut in quietly. "Have it your own way. I've tried the best I know how. So far as my actions are concerned—well, I do my work as well as any of your men, don't I?" He, too, got to his feet. "You got any kick on that score?"

"Not on yore work—no," Deming admitted grudgingly. He cast hurriedly about for some new complaint with which to obscure his own shortcomings. "But I don't like the way you spend yore time outside workin' hours."

"Meaning what?" Jeff stiffened slightly.

Deming faced away from his son, spoke over one shoulder. "This goin' to town so much is hard on hoss flesh—"

"Come to the point, Dad," Jeff said sharply. "It happens to be my own horse I'm ridin'. You're evading my question. Just what do you mean? I demand to know—"

"Oh, yo're demandin' now, are you?" John Deming laughed scornfully, whipping himself to a fury of hot rage. He swung squarely around to face his son, the pent-up accusation pouring forth in a heated torrent of words. "All right, I'll give you some man-talk. Yo're probably too *loco* for it to do you any good until you've come to yore senses, but the point is this—I don't like the idea of anyone with the Deming blood in his veins spendin' time with a greaser girl—"

"Careful, Dad," Jeff took one step toward his father. His sharp tones should have warned the elder Deming, but it was too late to dam the flow of angry words that rushed out.

"A greaser girl, that's all she is. If there wasn't more money sellin' blankets and such to tourists stoppin' off down in Gunsmoke City, she'd be where she belonged—over t'other side of the line, pattin' *tortillas* and raisin' a brood of black-eyed brats for some wuthless peon—"

"Stop, I tell you!"

Warned by something in Jeff's voice, the elder Deming subsided to a glowering silence. The two men stood eye to eye, fighting to hold their tempers, each realizing the breach was now beyond mending, each struggling to restrain the torrent of fresh abuse that rose to his lips. Jeff's fist raised, then with an effort he lowered it slowly to his side.

"Hah! Strike yore own flesh and blood, would you?" John Deming grated through set teeth.

Jeff gulped, holding his fist closely at his side. "I wish—I wish," he said ruefully, "you weren't my father. You'd take back everything you've said—in a hurry. I'll make this much clear: Lucita is not a greaser. She comes from old Spanish stock. There was a time when her family owned a good many hundred thousand acres in California—"

"Too bad she didn't stay there then," Deming growled. "What's she doing this side of the Colorado?"

"I haven't asked her that."

"A heap of folks are wonderin' though," triumphantly.

51

"Let 'em wonder—or ask Lucita," Jeff retorted sharply. "I'm making this much clear: you've done a lot of boasting about the Deming blood. Well, Lucita's blood is as good as yours or mine—mebbe better. She's educated—"

"Old Spanish stock! Bah!" Deming laughed harshly. "I never yet saw a spick that didn't claim somethin' of the kind. I ain't never said anythin' before, but I know where you been goin' nights. Two and three nights every week." He sneered, "Chasin' down rumors, I suppose. More rot! Think I don't know how you spend yore time. Why don't you get a white—"

"Dad!" Jeff's face showed ashen in the gloom. His voice trembled as he said with some difficulty, "Don't—say—that—again."

Deming caught the warning glance in Jeff's eyes that told him his son couldn't stand much more without retaliation of some sort. He abruptly fell silent.

At the moment Jeff caught the sound of a footstep at the corner of the house. He moved quickly off the gallery, rounded a *palo verde* tree that blocked his progress and started along the side of the building. Ahead of him he could see a dark form hurrying through the darkness.

"Hey you!" Jeff called. "What you want?"

The figure stopped, turned back and proved to be Gabe Torango.

"I was just comin' to see yore paw, Jeff," the

substitute foreman explained. "Then I heard you talkin' and I didn't want to cut in—"

"What's up, Gabe?" the elder Deming's voice sounded from the corner of the house.

"Nothin' boss. Just wondered if there was any orders for to-morrow—anythin' special, that is."

"Why should there be?" John Deming asked sharply.

"Well, I was just wonderin', that's all," rather lamely.

"Quinn will be back tomorrow to do yore wonderin' for you," John Deming said shortly.

"That's just fine. Good-night." Torango resumed his progress toward the bunk-house.

Impatiently John Deming stepped back to the gallery. In a minute he was joined by Jeff. Jeff said, "Wonder what he was spyin' on us for?"

His father said sharply, "Who said he was spyin'?"

"What was he doin' there?"

"You heard him state his business, didn't you?"

"Yes, but I didn't believe him."

John Deming swore. "Yo're too damn suspicious, Jeff. Always lookin' for trouble."

"All right, mebbe I am," Jeff agreed wearily. He realized that his father was in no mood for sensible reasoning that night and could see no profit in further argument.

But John Deming wasn't inclined to relinquish his point. Taking Jeff's words of agreement as a sign of weakening, he plunged on, reopening the subject.

"All right, we won't mention the girl again, or her blood or what she is—"

"Dad!" Jeff protested.

"—what she is to you," Deming amended slyly, cooling down a trifle. "However," he continued doggedly, "you won't be denyin' that her father is suspected of bein' a cattle-thief—a bandit."

Jeff's lips tightened. "I won't deny there's suspicions in that direction, but there's no proof of the statement. We won't mention the matter any more."

The firm definite tones acted on the elder Deming like flame on excelsior. He flared, "There's one thing we will talk about then, and that's the way yo're wastin' yore time—regardless whether it's with a girl in town or not. At yore age you shouldn't have a thought in yore head, except what's best for the Rocking-D. You've got a good job here and yo're lettin' foolish suspicions and a kid dislike for yore foreman to stand in yore way—"

"If you think," Jeff exclaimed hotly, "that I'm goin' to take orders from Quinn Barker, and let him run me ragged, you're much mistaken, and the Rocking-D can go plumb to hell and Barker with it! Is that clear?"

Deming's face was apoplectic with rage. He sputtered and fumed and raved and cursed, only with difficulty finally managing to regain the normal use of his tongue.

"It's clear all right," he said ominously at last. "I been half expectin' you to take that attitude. I ain't surprised. Now, I'll tell you what I aim to do. You sort of figure that the Rocking-D will be yore property someday, whether you stay on or not. Well, I'll fool you. Either you'll settle down and work yore best under Quinn Barker, or I'll sell the outfit and you won't get one red cent!"

Deming's words, pronounced in the heat of anger, were unjust. Jeff shrugged his shoulders. "Go ahead. Sell if you like," he said quietly. "You know as well as I do that I'm willin' to work for anythin' I get. I've never given a thought, one way or the other, to having the Rocking-D when you passed on—"

"Don't lie! You figured it would be yours whether you worked for it or not."

Jeff said wearily, "Have it your own way, Dad. But I'll say this—you may have a harder job selling than you think. This is a pretty big spread and will take considerable money to handle. Money is rather tight right now. You won't find enough ready cash in all Smoky Range to—"

"I already got a buyer. Goin' to sell to him too," Deming stated triumphantly. "Seein' you and me can't get along friendly, I might just as well sell out. Been sort of figurin' on goin' up to Montana. I've got friends up there that I haven't seen for years. They've been writin' frequent about money to be made in minin' copper. Mebbe I'll go into minin', start out afresh and try and forget the ingratitude of a son—"

"That's not fair, Dad."

Deming snorted. "Mebbe not from yore viewpoint, but I know different. One thing's certain—I ain't intendin' to have the worry of operatin' a cow outfit on my mind, if my own flesh and blood ain't enough interested to lend a hand." Anger vibrated in his voice. "By Gawd! I'll show you if you can run things to suit yoreself. You won't get one two-bit piece when I receive the money!"

Jeff felt sick at heart over the whole business. "Let's not scrap, Dad," struggling to hold his voice level. "Probably it'll be best if you do sell out. You'll find new interests in Montana and old friends. That's fine. You're mistaken if you think I want any of the money. Go ahead. Sell. You deserve a rest. . . . Got any objectin' to tellin' me who the buyer is?"

"Nope," crustily. "Quinn Barker. We talked it over a couple of weeks ago—"

"Barker!" Incredulous flames leaped in Jeff's eyes. "Barker? Him? . . ." Jeff laughed shortly. "All right. It's none of my business, but I'd sure like to know where he expects to get the money. He sure didn't save that much out of his wages—"

"You don't even know the selling price—"

"I know you wouldn't let it go cheap—can't imagine you selling for less than a hundred thousand—"

"Hundred and ten," Deming snapped. "Quinn is payin' twenty-five thousand, cash down. I'm taking his note for the balance, note secured by the property and to be paid off in annual installments—"

Jeff whistled softly. "I crave to know where Barker could raise twenty-five thousand dollars," he said evenly. "Hefty and Three-Star were tellin' me that you didn't get the gathering you expected the last three falls. Calves *and cows* not up to expected tally—"

"Now, look here, Jeff," Deming exploded. "I won't listen to talk like that. Barker ain't a cattle-thief. Sure, I've had stock rustled from time to time, but any large outfit is shore to have losses. Barker had money when he first come here—"

"You got proof of that?"

"I saw his bank-book last week, the first entry datin' back to when he first signed on with the Rocking-D. He's got more now than he had then. At the time I hired him, he told me that he only aimed to work for me until he could get a chance to learn the country. Then he was goin' to start an iron of his own. I'm lucky that he stuck with me this long, but"—Deming chuckled sourly—"I wouldn't have signed him on my payroll, except that I had an idea I could make him stay on steady. And he has—"

"I'd like to bet, aces to tens, that if Barker has twenty-five thousand dollars," Jeff commented meaningly, "that he's already started to raise his own beef—with Rocking-D stock and help! . . . Well, it's your own funeral—and your outfit. Seein' I'm in no humor to work under Barker, I'll be pullin' out to-night. Hefty and Three-Star will be pullin' out with me. They feel the way I do about Barker—"

"Quinn will be glad to be shut of them, too," Deming snapped.

"Don't doubt it," Jeff acknowledged. "He's got rid of all our—your old crew, except those two, and hired a gang that looks pretty tough to me—"

"That's good sense," Deming growled. "A spread with a tough outfit ain't bothered much with rustlers."

"You've already admitted some losses."

"They could have been a heap worse," Deming grunted. He tried to change the subject. "Jeff, yo're just sore at Barker—"

"Damn right I am," Jeff said warmly. "I just wish I could make you see things my way for a short spell. You'd wake up and not trust a thing to Barker—"

"And you can mind yore own business," Deming rasped. "That's all I ask." His features settled into a steel-like mask. "You and Hennessey and Wilkins can come for yore time inside half an hour. I'll have yore wages for you!"

But Jeff hadn't waited to hear the final words. He was already rounding the *palo verde* tree at the corner of the house, walking sadly to the bunkhouse to pick up his few belongings and break the news to Three-Star and Hefty. Within the hour the three had silently saddled up and rode away from the Rocking-D, after a crusty farewell from John Deming in which no handclasps had been exchanged.

The following morning, upon Quinn Barker's arrival, John Deming had immediately opened the subject of Bob Deming's death, telling Barker of the accusations Jeff had made.

For a moment, when Deming had concluded, Barker remained silent. Deming said tersely, "Well, what about it, Quinn?"

Barker smiled, the smile expanded to a wide-lipped grin. "Do you mean to say that's news to you, John?"

"Shore was."

"Why, hell's bells! Look here, John, I didn't say anythin' at first, knowin' Bob's death was a tender subject. But I can't help laughin' now. I thought you knew about those old stories. Everybody in town's heard 'em, I reckon. You know how rumors grow. Well, I got enemies in Gunsmoke City. They'd like to make trouble for me. Mebbe I wouldn't have so many enemies if I looked the other way when it comes to countin' yore cattle. But I never could abide a cow-thief. I've made myself plain on that score, and because I've protected yore interests, there's a certain element that has done their best to get me jammed up. Hell! It's ridiculous. You know as well as I do that if there was any truth in the rumor that I had anythin' to do with Bob Deming's death, the proof would have come out long ago. You can't quiet an open and shut affair like that was."

"Reckon yo're right," Deming said. "I told Jeff that—"

"I'm standin' on my record," Barker pursued. " 'Bout five years of it, John. I've worked faithful for you. If I was a crook or murderer, you'd learned it long before this. Cripes! I won't even attempt to deny those rumors. They don't deserve that much attention."

"Exactly as I figured it." Deming seemed eager to have his own beliefs enforced.

"Where's Jeff now?" Barker went on. "I want to shake his hand, so's to show there's no hard feelin's."

Deming frowned darkly. "We had a few words last night. Jeff's left—along with Hennessey and Wilkins. He won't be back."

"That mean you'll sell?" Barker asked eagerly—just a shade too eagerly.

Deming nodded. "I'm ready to sell," he said

heavily. "When my own flesh and blood won't back me up, there's no use my goin' on with beef-raisin'. Yeah, I'm ready to sell, Quinn. I ain't sorry. Goin' to get out of the country altogether."

CHAPTER 4

Curly, bartender of the Warbonnet Saloon, Gunsmoke City's principal thirst emporium, glanced moodily at the few customers standing before the bar, then shifted his glance to gaze through a window at the muddy street. The rain had commenced with a slow, disagreeable drizzle just before daylight, and gradually increased until, at present, it was teeming a steady downpour with no signs of abatement.

A sudden gust rattled the door, and for a few minutes it was impossible to see through the sheets of water that beat against the window-panes.

"Set up the drinks, Señor Curly," came a soft voice from the rear end of the bar. "Theese time the refreshments are on me."

The speaker was Otón Madero, suspected of being the head of a gang of Mexican bandits. Despite these suspicions, people liked Madero, as a general thing. He was generous with his money, cool-nerved, and always the gentleman. Bandit he may have been, but if so, he confined his operations, so far as could be ascertained, to the country south of the Mexican Border. Considerable of his time was spent in Gunsmoke City—no one knew why, though it was thought that the residence of his daughter, Lucita, in town probably had something to do with it. At the same time, it was rumored he owned a large *ranchero* in the State of Sonora.

Madero was a rather handsome, smiling man, with a lean, lithe form, olive complexion and dark hair commencing to gray at the temples. He was clad in the clothing of a typical Mexican dandy: deep red velvet trousers, bell-bottomed and tight across the hips; a short jacket of the same material, steeple-crowned sombrero heavily embroidered with gold thread. On his feet were high-heeled riding-boots of hand-tooled leather, equipped with silver-inlaid spurs with gigantic rowels. His shirt was of fine white linen. In strange contrast to this elaborate costume was the well-worn cartridge-belt and holster at his slim hips, the latter holding a walnut-butted Colt gun.

If the folks of Gunsmoke City liked Madero, they adored his daughter. Lucita operated a small curio shop on the main street, and such tourists as stopped in town, between stages, bought lavishly of her *chimayo* blankets, Mexican pottery, and Indian jewelry. Father and daughter had arrived in Gunsmoke City less than a year before, but already they had been accorded a respect on a plane commanded by any of the town's citizens—and considerably more than some.

The door of the Warbonnet suddenly burst inward, the wind driving gusts of rain to form tiny pools on the pine flooring. Trigger Texas rocked in, swearing, water dripping from his wide-brimmed sombrero.

"Nice day," Texas commented, wiping his face with a dirty bandanna.

"*Si*, for the mud-turtle," Madero smiled dubious agreement. "You are just in time to join us in a drink, Señor Texas."

Texas said, "Thanks," and took a place at the bar. Whisky was poured and consumed, glasses replaced on the long counter.

"What brings you in to town, Texas?" queried the 90-Bar puncher."

"I rode in with Barker," Texas explained briefly. "We got soaked. Hell of a day to ride any place."

"How about it, Texas?" Curly asked, replacing bottles on his back bar. "Is there any truth in the report that John Deming is selling the Rocking-D to Quinn Barker?"

Texas nodded. "It's so. They're aimin' to put the deal through right shortly. Barker's over to the bank now drawin' out his money. Deming will be in later—"

"Hell," someone interposed, "the bank's closed, ain't it?"

Curly consulted an old brass watch. "It's just three o'clock now," he announced. "Reckon Barker got in before they closed the door—"

At that moment the door opened, admitting

further gusts of wet wind. Quinn Barker entered, bearing in his right hand a small satchel. He strode across to the bar, handed the satchel to Curly. "Put that in yore safe for me, will you, Curly? It's a tidy sum of cash money."

The barkeep nodded, knelt before a small iron safe back of one end of the bar, and put the money away. Barker spoke to the other men in the room, then procuring a bottle of bourbon and followed by Texas, he retired to one of two back rooms, partitioned off from the bar for the convenience of those who wished to do their drinking in private or transact business deals.

Closing the door behind them, Texas and Barker seated themselves at a small table. Barker poured two glasses of whiskey.

"You got everythin' clear in yore mind, ain't you, Texas?" he queried anxiously. "I don't want any slip-up in the plans, y'know."

"There won't be no slip-up," Texas grunted, grinning nastily. "Here's the layout as I understand it—Deming comes here and you give him the twenty-five thousand, receivin' a bill of sale for the money, said bill statin' that you are givin' your note for eighty-five thousand dollars—balance on the purchase price—to be paid off in annual installments."

"Right so far," Barker nodded.

Texas continued, "I pull out of town ahead of Deming, wait until he comes along with the money, which same I take, together with your note, as soon as I've plugged him—"

"You've got it down pat, Trigger," Barker complimented.

"I'm not through yet," Texas growled. "I don't figure for you to forget that my share is half of that money—twelve thousand, five hundred. Also, I'm to have a cut in Rocking-D profits when you get to operatin'. You see, Quinn, I don't want any slip-up either."

"There won't be," Barker said coldly. "You'll get your money. But don't try to double-cross me. I'll get you if you do. Play square with me and yo're made. The way I got things worked out, we'll get the whole outfit without payin' a cent. I figure to give Scar Tonto and Bulldog Higgins a cut on the proceeds with us two. They're old friends and are in on our plans. The rest of the boys don't get a cent extra. They'll have to be satisfied with good wages."

"I don't see why Scar and Bulldog should get anythin'," Texas grumbled. "Here, I do the dirty work and them two that's supposed to be so good with guns—"

"Listen, Texas," Barker said menacingly, "I made these plans. You ought to be glad I let you in on the scheme—"

"Just the same, I don't like—"

"Damn yore likes and dislikes," Barker snarled. "The plans are all made. Are you goin' through with 'em or aren't you? If you aren't you've got to face me—" and one hand dropped ominously to the butt of his six-shooter.

"All right, Quinn," Texas said hastily. "You're right. I don't want any fight with you. Just forget that I mentioned anythin'."

"That's better," Barker grunted, relaxing. "You play my way and you'll get rich. Buck me and you'll get—a slug of lead."

"But I get half that twenty-five thousand right off the bat, don't I?"

"Told you once you did, didn't I? I don't break my word."

Texas nodded. There was silence between the two men for a few moments, then he asked, "Have you figured that young Deming might make some trouble for you?"

Barker laughed shortly. "Not a chance. In the first place it will look like a legal deal. In the second, he's sore at his old man. They ain't hardly on speakin' terms. That quarrel Torango overheard settled things for those two for all time. That's two weeks back. If John Deming had wanted to patch things up, he'd have took steps to do it by this time. But he's through with Jeff. Said so to me more'n once. Which condition suits our plans right down to the ground."

"Things is shore shapin' up our way all right," Texas agreed.

Barker resumed talk of the plan: "Now, listen,

Trigger. Deming won't get in town to complete our deal until around supper-time. Before I left the ranch I spent some time with Deming's horse—"

"Deming's horse?" Texas looked puzzled.

Barker grinned nastily. "One of the shoes needed a little attention. Betcha ten bucks Deming's pony goes lame before he gets here. That's goin' slow him up a heap—"

"What's the idea?"

"The deal won't be completed until evenin'. That will give you darkness to work in. With this rain, and all, you ain't li'ble to run into anybody that might get curious. Everythin' is comin' our way."

"What you aimin' to do?"

"So far as anybody will know, I'll be stayin' in town tonight."

"Hotel?"

Barker nodded. "The rain will give me a good excuse for not goin' back to the ranch. I already got my room. First floor, facin' on an alleyway. When I go out to supper I'll tie my bronc in the alley close by. Some time after I go to my room for the night I'll slip out my window, ride to the Rocking-D—"

"Better not travel by way of Crooked Pass," Texas said meaningly.

"Don't worry. I'll take the long road around. I don't crave to be anywhere near John Deming's

68

corpse. Lucky for us, Deming always insists on taking the Crooked Pass route—"

Texas prompted, "After you get to the Rocking-D, what?"

Barker explained, "I know where Deming keeps the deed to the outfit. I'll get that, then ride like hell back to the hotel, and slip through the window of my room. Then I'll fix up another bill of sale. I been practisin' John Deming's signature for a long spell now. I won't have any trouble signin' his name good enough to fool anyone who might get inquisitive. You watch my smoke, Trigger, and you'll see a right pretty deal put across."

Texas frowned, "I don't see any chance of a slip-up, Quinn. At the same time—" He hesitated.

"What's eatin' on you now, Trigger?"

"I wish we knowed what young Deming will do. Ever since that day, last spring, when he shot you, I been tryin' to figure what way he'd jump if there was any kind of a blow-up. I'm statin' frank, I can't dope him out. It don't seem natural that he'd just ride off and let somebody grab what would, by rights, be his property someday. I'm just wonderin' if he ain't got some scheme of his own."

"I ain't worryin' about him," Barker laughed confidently. "You just follow my instructions and everythin' will work out without a hitch. The plan's unbeatable. I know what I'm talkin' about.

It's all up to you. Do yore part and we won't have a worry. But don't bungle things, Trigger."

"I won't bungle 'em," Texas promised.

Barker rose to his feet. It was growing dark in the little back room now.

"You goin' to light that lamp?" Texas pointed to an oil-lamp standing on a shelf on one wall.

Barker shook his head. "C'mon, we'll get back to the bar. There's goin' to be a heap of excitement break loose on this range before many hours. When it does, we don't want anybody rememberin' that you and me spent a long time here carryin' on a private conversation."

CHAPTER 5

Curly was just lighting the swinging oil-lamps that illuminated the barroom when Barker and Texas returned to the bar.

At a quarter to seven the door was shoved open, and Jeff Deming, accompanied by Three-Star Hennessey and Hefty Wilkins, stepped inside. Their slickers were shiny-wet under the lights from the oil-lamps, and the trio stamped mud from their high-heeled boots as they strode to the bar.

Jeff and his companions nodded to Curly, Madero and three or four others, but completely ignored the presence of Barker and Trigger Texas. Barker's face flushed crimson with anger, his eyes darted a glance of hate at Jeff.

"Ain't seen you three lately," Curly greeted, as he took the orders. "Where you been the past few days?"

Jeff and his friends were shaking water from their sombreros and slickers. Jeff said, "Hefty and Three-Star and myself have been takin' a little vacation. We've been livin' in that old shack up above Crooked Pass. It made a good headquarters while we did a mite of huntin'. Mostly though we been loafin' around, smokin' and eatin' and wonderin' what we'd do next."

"Make up your minds?" Curly asked, sliding glasses and a bottle along the bar.

Jeff shrugged his lean shoulders as he poured a neat "two fingers" of bourbon. "We ain't certain yet what we'll do. We may head up through Colorado. Nice country thataway. A change of scenery don't hurt anybody either."

Three-Star cast a quick meaning glance at Barker. "And a change of scenery is somethin' I crave," he stated gravely. "This country is gettin' plumb overrun with skunks."

Barker, still smarting under the manner in which Jeff had ignored him, swung away from the bar and approached Jeff.

"Deming," Barker rasped, "you and yore pals can vacate that cabin above Crooked Pass after to-night. That's on Rocking-D holdin's, and I'm damn particular who stays there. I suppose you know who's buyin' the outfit—"

"I've heard the bad news," Jeff said steadily. "Howsomever, it's none of my business."

"Damn right it ain't!" Barker exclaimed triumphantly. "Just the same yo're sore as hell at the way you lost out, ain't you? And I'm warnin' you—keep off Rocking-D property from now on. I'll have a man posted to throw lead at trespassers—"

Jeff smiled contemptuously. "Your warnin' came too late, Barker. We already moved out. Won't be goin' back."

A flicker of sudden relief showed momentarily in Barker's and Texas's eyes.

Jeff went on, "Yep, we brought our stuff into town this afternoon. And, Barker, don't get the idea I'm sore about Dad sellin' the Rocking-D. What he does with his property is his own business. As I said before, it's not my affair." A reckless expression entered his features as he added softly, "I'm doin' a heap of wonderin', though, just where your money is comin' from, Barker."

Barker stiffened. "Meanin' just what?" he demanded.

Jeff faced the man squarely. "Meanin'," he explained in no uncertain tones, "that everybody knows the Rocking-D had been shy a heap of stock at beef round-up and spring brandin' the last few years!"

Barker's eyes blazed. "You suspectin' me of stealin' stock—"

"I'm not suspectin' you," Jeff shook his head. "I'm *accusin'* you!"

Barker's face paled. He took one retreating step. "If you ain't got proof, those are fightin' words," he said in ugly accents.

"I ain't got proof," Jeff confessed, then threw his challenge, "but I'm sure admittin' they're fightin' words. Are you game to do anythin' about it, or did I give you all the leadin' you needed last spring?"

A tense silence suddenly descended on the Warbonnet, broken only by the shrieking of the storm and howling of wind outside. With the passing of moments there came a gradual retreat of customers from the bar. At one end Otón Madero lounged gracefully as before, his dark features showing a distinct interest in the proceedings while he dawdled over a small glass of *aguardiente*, refusing to budge even though he was well within gunshot range should lead commence to fly.

Jeff was standing easily facing Barker, one elbow on the bar rail. Barker stood about three yards away. Hefty and Three-Star hadn't shifted position. One stood at Jeff's left, the other a short distance from Barker and to one side.

Apparently no one had noticed Trigger Texas, who was edging around to take up a position behind the big-bellied cast-iron stove which stood, now cold and rusty, in the centre of the bar-room.

Curly, the bartender, finally broke the tense silence:

"Looky here, you hombres," he growled, "if you're aimin' to spill any lead, g'wan outside where the rain will keep your shootin'-irons from gettin' overheated. I don't crave, nohow, to have the Warbonnet shot up. Furnishin's cost money—"

Jeff replied, without taking his eyes from

Barker, "Curly, I'll pay for any damage that's done. The next move is up to Barker." Jeff had thrown his slicker back and hooked thumbs into cartridge-belt, while he stood quietly waiting.

Barker's face was ghastly. "I—I don't want to fight with you now, Deming," he faltered. "I got too much at stake. You can't block the deal me and yore paw is puttin' through by proddin' me into a gun-fight. I ain't rollin' lead tonight. Some other time—"

"By Gawd! I'll call his bluff!" yelled Trigger Texas from his position behind the stove, where he was well shielded from any lead that Jeff might throw. Already Texas's gun-barrel was swinging through the air. And then, as Jeff made a swift move to one side, reaching for his gun, he saw the lean, red-clad form of Otón Madero interpose himself before Texas and shove a six-shooter against the badman's middle.

"Put down the gun, please, Señor Texas," Madero was ordering in his velvety tones. "I have been watching you. So! You would take advantage of the Señor Deming, and make the shot before he is prepar' to face you. *Valgame Dios!*" Madero laughed silently with some scorn. "Ah, that ees ver' bad. Clean gun-play I can endure—but murder—no. Put down the gun, I say."

"Damn you, greaser!" Texas snarled. "This ain't yore business. I'll—"

"You weel put down the gun," Madero pursued swiftly, "and, also, make the apology for that 'gresair' word what you employ so careless. Queek! The apology." The words were enforced by a sudden prodding of Madera's gun against Texas's middle.

Abruptly Texas wilted and holstered his gun. "Reckon I spoke out of turn," he mumbled. "I'm plumb sorry, Madero."

Madero smiled, showing white, even teeth. "Your apology is accep', Señor Texas." He holstered his gun. "I'm through weeth you now."

"But I'm not," Jeff said sternly, backing away and holding his arms well from sides. "Texas, you've made a bad play. Carry it through. Fill yore hand!"

Instead of drawing, the badman threw his hands into the air. He commenced backing away, shaking his head nervously. "You got me wrong, Jeff, old man—"

"It's the only way anybody could get *you,*" Jeff snapped.

"I didn't mean no harm," Texas pleaded. "You and Madero just jumped to conclusions—"

"If Señor Madero hadn't jumped fast it'd been my conclusion all right," Jeff said grimly. "Cut out the palaver, Texas. You wanted action. Go for your iron."

But Texas refused to fight. He kept his arms well in the air. "I ain't makin' any fight tonight,

Deming. You got too many friends here. But some other time, when things are even, I'll—"

"You lousy coyote," Jeff spoke contemptuously, "if you won't draw, I can't make you. But I'll run you out of Gunsmoke City, s'help me. Get goin'! Next time you cut my trail I'll be slingin' lead through your filthy carcass. Now, get!"

Without a word Texas turned and hurried through the doorway into the dripping night. The door slammed at his heels.

Jeff turned back to Madero. "I'm thanking you a heap for stopping that snake," he said earnestly, extending his hand. "He might have spelt my finish."

"*Gracias*, Señor Deming. Eet was nozzeeng. I did not wan' to see you murder' by that skonk—is all. I knew you and your pardners were giveeng your attention—elsewhere."

Barker's face reddened as he turned abruptly away from the bar and started for one of the private back rooms. "Curly," he snapped over his shoulder, "I'll be back here. Tell John Deming where I am when he arrives."

Jeff started forward to stop the man, then decided to let the matter drop. Curly nodded assent. Barker disappeared in the back room, banging the door behind him. In a few more minutes, with the assistance of Curly's services, conversation again became normal.

The men at the bar were just emptying glasses when John Deming arrived. He shook the rain from his slicker and vouchsafed a brief nod that included his son with the rest of the customers. Then he spoke directly to Jeff:

"I just ran into Texas down the street. He told me a few things. You been fightin' again, eh?"

Jeff said quietly, "It might be a good idea to get both sides of the argument before passing judgment—"

"I don't need to hear both sides," John Deming cut in sharply. "You've got a bad streak in yore make-up—just like yore brother Bob had. Take my advice and mend yore ways, boy, or you'll be endin' up at the end of a hangman's noose one of these days—that or somethin' worse. You better make a fresh start right soon."

"I'm living my own life," Jeff said a bit bitterly. "That's more than you'd let me do."

Deming frowned, face clouding up. He started a sharp reply, then checked the hot words that rose to his lips. Abruptly he turned away and asked Curly, "Where's Barker gone to? Texas told me he was waitin' for me here."

"Yeah, he is," Curly replied. "Waitin' in that back room, Mister Deming," accompanying the words with a gesturing thumb.

A pregnant silence followed Deming's departure. No one wanted to mention the sale of the Rocking-D in Jeff's presence, yet all knew that thoughts of the property transfer were surely uppermost in the young cowboy's mind.

Jeff said awkwardly at last, "Reckon I'll take a little walk."

CHAPTER 6

Jeff stood a few moments under the broad wooden awning that fronted the Warbonnet Saloon, gazing out into the rain-beaten street.

Two riders took form in the gloom and splashed up to the hitch-rack, their ponies' hoofs sucking mud at every step.

Jeff recognised Scar Tonto and Bulldog Higgins, two of the Rocking-D hands.

"Oh, it's you, eh, Jeff," from Higgins.

Jeff didn't reply. There was something ominous in the air, a distinct presentiment of evil that he couldn't shake off, but exactly what it was he couldn't determine. He hurried down the street to Lucita Madero's curio shop.

In the back was a small door which led to living quarters which Lucita shared with her father, Otón Madero—during those occasions when the elder Madero chose to remain in town. It had been noted that he was away much of the time.

To the right of the door, built into the corner of the shop, a small fireplace shed a warm glow. A few feet from the fire Lucita sat writing at a small table of oak manufacture. The girl glanced up as Jeff entered the shop, then quickly thrust the paper on which she'd been writing into a table drawer, and placed her pen on the blotter before her. Rising to her feet, she smiled a welcome and stepped forward, both hands outstretched.

"Jeff!"

Jeff smiled. "I thought I'd drag some dampness in here."

"Throw your slicker over there," the girl gestured toward a low wooden bench. "Water can't hurt that."

Lucita Madero was a tall girl, with a slim, well-rounded form. Her hair, the blackness of black ink, was parted in the centre and drawn low at the back of her neck. Her eyes were a soft, velvety brown that looked directly at—and into—a person. The girl's features were exceptionally good, showing character rather than mere beauty. Her skin was olive-tinted, flushed with the rosy colour of natural health.

At present Lucita was dressed in a loose Indian blouse of dark red velvet, a deep green corduroy skirt and moccasins of fawn-skin. A silver bracelet encircled her left wrist. A necklace of silver and turquoise was about her throat. There weren't any rings on her slim fingers. There was a certain vitality, strength, about the girl. And yet, to Jeff, she seemed more wholly feminine tonight than at any time he had known her. His thoughts strayed back to other days when she had sat a horse's back at his side when the two took long rides. Those days she had worn riding-boots and faded blue overalls, with her dark hair in a bandanna covering. Lucita could ride as well as any man Jeff had ever known. He had seen her handle a lariat once or twice. Jeff's glance roved to the holstered six-shooter and cartridge-belt hanging above the fireplace. Lucita could shoot too.

The girl's abilities in these lines had seemed strange to Jeff Deming when he first came to know her, but as Lucita had explained, "It all comes natural enough when you're brought up to it. You see, father had always wanted a son. Mother died before that could happen, and he had my bringing up. There's much to be done on a large *rancho*, and father had no time for womanly foibles. And so I was educated in man things—mostly—back in those California days. Later—when it was too late to breed out the horse and cow knowledge I'd learned—we came east. Here and there I picked up an education. You know, Jeff," the girl had added laughingly, "if the Rocking-D ever got shorthanded, I could hold down a job for your father if he'd take me on. I really could, you know."

All this had been months before, long before Jeff had ever dreamed of leaving the Rocking-D and quarrelling with his father. Now, as he stood talking to the girl, her words swept back to him with a rush that brought a twinge of pain with the thought. Now, it appeared, Lucita could never be asked to go to the Rocking-D. While Jeff had said nothing yet, it had long been his dream someday to ask Lucita to share, as his bride, the Rocking-D Ranch.

"Jeff," Lucita finally broke the silence, "something's bothering you."

"Is it?" Jeff evaded with a slight smile.

The girl wouldn't be put off. "Is it the sale of the Rocking-D?"

"You know about it, eh?"

"Dad told me," the girl replied. "The news is pretty generally known and has been talked about for some time. Quinn Barker has been saying he was going to take over the place. Dad says you quarreled with your father."

"I reckon I did."

"What about?"

"It doesn't matter now." Jeff wasn't meeting the girl's eyes. "Mostly I got plumb weary of bein' treated like a shorthorn, and—"

"And what?" as Jeff hesitated.

"That's about all, I reckon."

"Jeff," the girl spoke with swift intuition, "did I have anything to do with it?"

"You?" Jeff laughed carelessly. "Why should you?"

"Don't put me off, Jeff. Did I?"

Jeff didn't reply.

Lucita pursued, "Your father objected to our being together, didn't he?"

Jeff flushed. "Well, sort of," he admitted

reluctantly. "I reckon it would have been the same with any girl though—"

"No, it wouldn't," Lucita shook her head. "It's because I'm Spanish. Oh, I know, Jeff. Don't deny it—"

"He's stubborn as a mule," Jeff growled. "I've tried to make him understand you're as Americanized as any girl we know of—that your people were the real thing back in California and your blood better than that of the Demings. I told him you had holdings down in Mexico that had come straight from a Spanish king—say, how did you know your name had been brought into it?"

"Quinn Barker's been talking. I suppose your father—"

Jeff said wrathfully, "I reckon Barker needs a gunning."

"Never mind that; you'd only get into trouble, Jeff. You know"—the girl smiled softly—"it doesn't bother me one bit. Except that I'm sorry your father and I couldn't be friends."

"So am I," Jeff said moodily. "You see, 'Cita, I'd hoped someday to ask you to come to the Rocking-D as my—my—well—"

"Yes?" Lucita prompted.

Jeff didn't reply for a moment. "It doesn't matter much," he said miserably, "not now. The ranch is passing out of Deming hands. I don't so much mind losing it—what it might have meant to me—to us—someday, as I do the thought of Barker getting the old place. Shucks! I can make my own way. I'll get money. You watch my smoke, 'Cita—"

"I certainly will."

"And when I get said money, well—" Jeff grinned suddenly, thrusting other thoughts behind him, "—I'll finish what I stopped myself from sayin' a few moments back."

"For that," and the girl's brown eyes were steady, "I'm sorry, Jeff. You see, money wouldn't make any difference."

Jeff nodded. He saw the girl's eyes were shiny-moist. One of her slim, tanned hands reached out and touched Jeff's arm. "I can wait, Jeff," she said softly.

The door of the shop opened suddenly and Otón Madero entered, shedding water in all directions as he doffed his slicker. "Ah, eet is a customer—no?"

Jeff said "No," and laughed, adding, "you got to have money to be a customer. Money is something I haven't."

"Always," Madero returned courteously, "you are welcome in Lucita's little shop—money or no. But is always theese way. Many *vaqueros* come to theese shop, but few buy. Always they like to talk. Excep' when my 'Cita ees not here. Then, they do not stay. I'm theenk maybee Lucha have something to do weeth eet—No?"

Lucita joined in the laughter that greeted the words.

Jeff said, "Speaking of customers. I've often wondered why you chose Gunsmoke City for your shop. There aren't many tourists come through here. The town itself buys but little. Doesn't look to me like the business you get would support a shop."

"We manage to get along," Lucita said briefly.

"Well, I'm not aimin' to be curious," Jeff said, "only I don't see—"

Lucita repeated, "We manage to get along." Her manner had suddenly changed.

"You can't tell me," Jeff said, "that you operate at a profit."

"That doesn't worry me!" The words were short.

Jeff looked puzzledly at the girl, then flushed to the roots of his hair. "Reckon you'll have to excuse me," he said awkwardly. "I didn't mean to be inquisitive."

Lucita shrugged her shoulders. "It's nothing, Jeff. We liked the town. We settled here. If I don't make money, I don't lose any either. Let's forget it."

Silence descended on the pair, Jeff mentally cursing himself for talking too much, and at the same time wondering what there was in the subject to make Lucita so secretive. Old stories of Madero's activities came to mind. If it were true that the man were a bandit, then the curio shop would afford an excuse for his staying in Gunsmoke City. But what of Lucita? What part did she play in the situation? A lump rose in Jeff's throat. Somehow, a wall of restraint had grown between himself and the girl. The presentiment of evil that had weighted his thoughts a short time before again returned to hover, like a waiting buzzard, over his consciousness. It was something he couldn't shake off.

The talk turned to various subjects. Finally, Madero mentioned the trouble with Barker and Trigger Texas in the Warbonnet.

Lucita looked startled. "Jeff, you didn't tell me anything of that," she reproached.

"Wasn't much to tell," Jeff said evenly, "except that your dad saved my life, I reckon."

Lucita insisted on details and Madero supplied them. A look of fear crept over the girl's fine features as he talked. Finally, when he had finished, Lucita said: "I don't like it, Jeff. One way or another Barker will try to even the score with you. And he won't fight fair. If I were only sure that—" She broke off suddenly and looked at her father.

Some sort of swift message passed between the two, then Madero said suavely, "One can be sure of nozeeng, 'Cita. Eet is bes' not to speculate on anyzeeng."

"Sure of what?"

Lucita shrugged her shoulders. "As Dad says—

87

it is nothing," she replied shortly, then changed the subject. "I think it a shame that Barker should get the Rocking-D property."

"He's payin' for it," Jeff reminded.

Madero put in, "With Lucita I agree. Eet ees not right. You, Jeff, are the rightful heir. The land should stay in the family. Were I your age, in your boots, I might—"

He paused.

"Well?"

Madero laughed softly. "Always I go off on the tangent. Me, I should do nothing, I'm guess. Still, I could wish there were not so many laws. Eef I were not the law-abiding citizen, I would advise Jeff to take what is rightfully his, but I would not do that. Eet would only make trouble. But still, I could wish there were not so many laws. *Caracoles*! I talk on and on like one who is empty of head. Pay no attention."

He rose suddenly and went to get his slicker and high-peaked hat.

"You're going out, Dad?" Lucita asked.

"*Si*, my 'Cita," Madero nodded, shrugging his form into the slicker.

"Where?" the girl asked.

Madero smiled. "Would you ask the south wind where it goes when it ceases blowing? Already I hav' blow too much. I talk but I do not say anyzeeng. I must get out and air the cobwebs of my brain. *Adios*!"

The door closed behind him. For a moment they saw his form faintly through the rain-streaming window at the front of the shop, then he was gone.

Jeff laughed. "Yore paw shore makes up his mind plumb pronto, 'Cita."

The girl nodded. "Dad is like that. He's the most restless man I've ever known. Always on the go. I've known him to leave abruptly like that and then not return for two or three days."

"My gosh! Where does he go?"

"You'll have to ask him," Lucita replied. "I gave up looking for an answer to that question long ago."

Silence again fell. Embers glowed dully in the fireplace. A chill had seemed to steal into the little shop. Jeff tried to catch the girl's eyes with his own, but she managed to evade him.

Jeff said heavily, "It's getting late. Time to close up, I reckon."

"Don't hurry," Lucita said. "It's not late at all. Why do you say that, Jeff?"

Jeff didn't look at the girl. "Late for me, anyway," he replied. "I've got into the habit of rollin' in early. . . ."

Meanwhile, the sale of the Rocking-D had been put through. John Deming stood in the doorway of the Warbonnet holding a satchel containing twenty-five thousand dollars, in coin and paper money, and a note, signed by Quinn Barker, for the balance of the purchase price. In return, Quinn Barker had gained a bill of sale stating the money paid and the conditions of the transaction. Both documents had been written by Barker at Deming's dictation. They were properly signed, with the names of Scar Tonto and Bulldog Higgins added as witnesses to the signatures. The deal had been handled in the privacy of the Warbonnet's back room.

Deming frowned about the room as he buttoned his slicker, jammed down his sombrero and started out. Then, on a sudden thought, he turned back toward the bar, saying:

"Curly, if anybody should ask for me, tell 'em I'll be out to the Rocking-D till the end of the week. The new owner is allowin' me to stay 'til I get ready to leave. I'm tellin' you in case anybody should want to see me about anythin'."

" 'Right, Mister Deming," the barkeep nodded. "I'll remember. Good-night." Curly knew that Deming had referred to Jeff when he used the word "anybody."

Deming gruffly said good-night and pushed out into the rain. The door closed at his heels.

Curly turned back to the bar, swept up in one motion a line of empty glasses and dropped them into a tub of water under the counter. Then he turned to Barker, Tonto and Higgins who still stood at the bar, and asked, "Ain't nobody goin' with Mister Deming? He might get stuck up and lose that money. It ain't right, him travellin' alone."

Barker laughed shortly. "Nobody's going to try to hold up John Deming. He's too powerful in the Smoky Range country for anybody to dare try it. He'd make it too hot for 'em. I reckon John can take care of himself. He don't need a bodyguard. Me and Scar and Bulldog is aimin' to sleep in style at the hotel tonight. Too wet to be out. 'Sides, I want to order a bill of goods, first thing in the morning, and there ain't no use of makin' an extra trip. . . . Curly, call up the house: the new owner of the Rocking-D is buyin' the drinks. Drink hearty, hombres, drink hearty!"

CHAPTER 7

Three-Star and Hefty were waiting for Jeff when he emerged from Lucita's shop. A short distance down the street they caught sight of John Deming. A yellow flood of light, emanating from the windows of the Warbonnet Saloon, threw into bold relief the elder Deming's slickered form at the hitch-rack, mounting his horse. Through the slanting arrows of rain, Jeff saw his father lift the satchel of money to the saddle in front of him, then wheel the horse and move off down the street.

Jeff watched his father merge with the wet darkness of the roadway and gradually fade from sight. A lump swelled in Jeff's throat.

"I reckon," he said slowly, "the old outfit belongs to Quinn Barker now."

"Hell of a note," Hefty growled.

"Seems thataway," Jeff nodded. "I don't so much mind the place being sold as I do the thought of a snake like Barker gettin' what my mother helped to build up. She sure helped Dad in the early days when they were getting started. I remember, when I was a little tyke, her tellin' me how she helped Dad fight off a party of Apaches that had hit out on the warpath. Dad would never have sold the place if she'd been alive—"

Three-Star cursed softly. "Damn that Barker.

I'll bet he never come by that money honest. I don't see where he could get twenty-five thousand dollars—"

"Good Cripes!" Jeff cut in abruptly. "I just happened to think that that's a heap of money for Dad to be packing with him. He should have put the deal through in the daytime, so he could put the money in the bank—either that or insisted on Barker paying with a check." He laughed a trifle bitterly. "Oh, well, it's none of my business. Dad has told me enough to keep my nose out of his affairs." He repeated, "It's none of my business—I guess. Still, I don't like the thought. . . . Shucks! No sense of my botherin' about it. Let's go get a cup of coffee and a hunk of pie down to the restaurant."

"That's an idea," Hefty agreed.

The three moved diagonally across the street, picking their way around mud puddles, to reach the doorway of the Kansas City Café.

Fifteen minutes later, Jeff rose suddenly from his stool at the long counter of the restaurant, and commenced to fasten his slicker.

"What now?" Three-Star asked. "What's yore rush?"

"As I said before," Jeff explained, "it ain't none of my business, but I don't like the thought of Dad carrying so much money. I can't see why he didn't put it in a safe, some place. Somebody might stick him up."

"Nobody dare hold up John Deming—" Hefty commenced, then paused and continued, "I dunno. Mebbe they would, at that."

"That's the way it looks to me," Jeff nodded. "I'm goin' to get my horse and trail along after Dad—as a sort of unseen bodyguard. He'd get sore if he thought I was following him, so I won't make any attempt to catch up. We quarreled, but I can't forget he's my father. I'd hate to see anything happen to him."

"We'll go with you," Three-Star suggested. He started to call the proprietor of the restaurant for the check, but Jeff stopped him. The proprietor was out in the kitchen. There were no other customers in the place.

"No," Jeff said, "you boys stay and finish your coffee. No use you going out on a night like this. Besides—well, I'd sort of like to be alone for a spell. I want to think things over. Seeing the old place change hands got to me a lot worse than I figured it would. Understand what I mean, why I'd like to be alone?"

His two friends were quick to realise how Jeff felt and quickly dropped back to their seats.

Jeff pulled his sombrero low on his head. "If anybody should want to know where I am," he said awkwardly, "don't tell 'em I'm trailin' Dad. You see," he explained, "folks might think I was following along to talk him out of some of that money. You fellows know, as well as I, that

94

that's not the case. But other people might not understand. Fact is, Dad won't even learn that I'm following him."

The other two nodded. Jeff stepped out in a swirl of wind and rain, crossed the street and climbed into his wet saddle. Then he backed the horse and turned it in the direction he had last seen his father heading. . . .

And so John Deming, as he pounded along the trail to the Rocking-D, clutching firmly the satchel of money before him, wasn't aware of his son's intentions. The elder Deming never again expected to return to Gunsmoke City. The next few days he planned to spend at the Rocking-D, with Quinn Barker, clearing up odds and ends and turning over to the new owner the account books. When he got ready to leave for Montana, where he expected to renew old friendships, John Deming figured to ride, by horse, directly north to Puma Wells, a small stopping point on the T.N. & A.S. Railroad, and from there travel by train to his destination.

In view of such facts it had never occurred to Deming not to carry his money with him. From early manhood days he had been accustomed to travelling with large sums, from time to time. Now, though he had grown older and times had changed, he saw no reason for making any alterations in his habits.

There were two routes for reaching the

Rocking-D out of Gunsmoke City: one, the longer way, ran along level ground, but made a wide bend where it circled a point in the Arribas Mountains that bellied out into the range; the other trail led directly along a high ridge of the mountains and was easily negotiable, except at one point where the trail narrowed to the width of little more than a horse path, known as Crooked Pass. Here a rider must proceed with the utmost caution for a couple of hundred yards.

At its broadest point, Crooked Pass was not more than three yards wide. To westward of the trail was a sheer drop of three hundred feet to a rock-cluttered ravine far below. At the other side of the pass was a gradual rise covered with brush, huge granite boulders and splintered bits of broken rock. A short distance up this slope was the old shack where Jeff, Hefty and Three-Star had been staying.

By this time Deming had left Gunsmoke City far to the rear. The wind had slackened to some small extent, but continued to howl mournfully across the mountain peaks. Rain teemed down in descending torrents, drenching man and beast. Deming hunched lower in the saddle, drew his slicker closer about him and touched spurs to his mount.

They were ascending steeper grades now. The horse slowed pace of its own volition, after a time, to move out along the narrow ledge of rock that marked the approach to Crooked Pass.

For the first time, John Deming's mind commenced to fill with doubts regarding his actions in selling the ranch and toward Jeff.

"Now that it's done and over," he mused, "I kinda wish it could have been different. I wanted to do what was right by the boy, but he wouldn't let me. If we could only have talked without fightin', we might have got some place, but we couldn't. Jeff is too stubborn."

He set his lips firmly on the thought, half wondering whether or not he had given Jeff a square deal. The horse picked its way through the wet night. Gusts of wind flattened Deming's slicker against his lean form. Rain dripped continually from the brim of his hat. Far up the slope to Deming's right a tiny yellow gleam of light caught his eye. For a moment he didn't realise what it was, then he muttered:

"Oh, yeah, that old shack up there. Jeff was staying there with Hefty and Three-Star. Wonder if he's up there now. I got a notion to go up and see. I don't know though. We'd probably fight. Anyway, it seems like I heard Barker mentioned somethin' about him and Hefty and Three-Star movin' out. Reckon some hombre's holed up there until the rain stops—"

A sudden interruption from the brush at the side of the trail put a stop to Deming's cogitations.

"Stop right where you are!" a voice spoke

abruptly from the dripping darkness. The tones were thick, husky. Undoubtedly the speaker was attempting to disguise his voice. Further orders followed. "Hang tight to that money grip. Keep your other hand on the reins. Don't try to get away, or—"

"Or what?" John Deming snapped angrily.

"You know what, Deming," the ominous tones continued. "Just do as I say."

Deming had already pulled the horse to a halt. His eyes tried to pierce the gloom, but could make out nothing except a shadowy figure holding a gun. The next instant the man had slipped around to Deming's rear. Deming felt the muzzle of a gun jammed against his spine.

"Unfasten your slicker," came the next order. "Throw it back over your shoulders. Hurry it up!"

Deming obeyed. Rain soaked into his woolen clothing. He felt the bandit swiftly unbuckle his cartridge belt. A moment later, a faint crash coming from far below told Deming the bandit had hurled belt, holster and gun into the ravine beneath Crooked Pass.

"You're gettin' yourself into a heap of trouble—" Deming commenced.

"That's my lookout," came the swift reply. "You've had your way long enough around this range. I'm figurin' to run things for a spell. Now, you head your horse up yonder to that cabin. I left a light so you could see the path. Get goin' slow, you'll see the path in a second. You and me have got business to transact, and I don't aim to transact it here. Somebody might come along. Get goin' now. Don't make any false moves. I'm coverin' you with a cocked gun. And hold fast to that money grip."

Slowly Deming turned his horse up the side of the slope. The beast slipped once in the wet mud. The bandit swore, raised his gun.

"Don't do that again," he snapped.

"I can't help what the horse does—"

"You better!" the bandit laughed harshly.

Deming held the pony on a tight rein, the hold-up man following behind on foot. Rain struck the moving figures in savage gusts. The wind lifted to a screaming crescendo that tore viciously, at the stunted trees and brush on the mountain slope. The horse's slipping hoofs struggled for firm footing on the rain-drenched path.

Head erect, John Deming rode on toward the lighted cabin. He never dreamed that his life was in danger. Of one thing only was Deming certain: he was sure he had recognized the bandit's voice, and in that realisation a swift tinge of bitterness entered his being. . . .

CHAPTER 8

It was well after midnight when Quinn Barker departed from the Warbonnet Saloon and staggered uncertainly through the wet mud to his room at the hotel. Barker had bought round after round of drinks to celebrate his purchase of the Rocking-D.

Upon entering the hotel, the sleepy-eyed clerk informed him that Tonto and Higgins had gone to their room long since and were peacefully sleeping on the floor above. Barker's room was on the ground floor, at the back of the hotel, and there the clerk was forced to conduct him. The clerk started to unlock the door, but Barker angrily brushed him away and took the key from his hand and finally succeeded in letting himself into the room, while the offended clerk again retired to his office.

The room revolved dizzily as Barker shook his head to dispel the alcoholic cobwebs that entangled his brain. "Jus' damn fool, thash what I am," he muttered thickly, fighting to steady his whirling senses. "I should know better than to drink so mush, when I got make ride to the housh an' get that deed."

The problem of riding to the ranch house for the deed occupied his thoughts during several moments of hiccoughing silence. Then he thought of Texas and the job to be handled by that individual. "I wonder did Texas do it quick. Deming should be a corpse by thish time . . . hic! . . . wonder if I showed good sense trustin' Texas. He'd . . . hic! . . . rob his own mother if he . . . hic! . . . got chance. Don't know, though, what else I coulda done. Reckon Texas won't try to double-cross me. I'm too . . . hic! . . . slick for him. At that he might get that money and never come back . . . hic!"

The room was swaying from side to side now. Barker cursed futilely and nearly fell from his chair. Suppose Texas did steal that money after killing John Deming, and never returned to the Smoky Range country. It would be like Texas to do that sort of thing.

A vacuous grin appeared on Barker's loose features. "Don' care much if Trigger does light out with that cash money, after he's killed John Deming. I'd be shut of him then; he wouldn't dare come back here. And to get that money he'd have to kill Deming. Deming would fight to his last drop of blood, rather than . . . hic! . . . give it up. If Texas never . . . hic! . . . comes back here, it'll save me splittin' profits with him. I'd . . . hic! . . . have the Rocking-D . . . all to myself. . . . I dunno though . . . hic! . . . thash lot of money. Twenty-five thousand dollars ish twenty-fi' . . . hic! . . . twenty-fi' . . . hic! twenty-fi' . . . hic! . . . twent . . ."

The words ended in a long snore. Barker put out one unsteady hand, toppled from his chair and fell across the bed. For a moment he threshed about, getting his legs straight, then his body sagged into limp relaxation. He snored loudly. The lamp on the dresser burned with a steady flame.

No one sleeps so soundly as an intoxicated man. Thus it was Barker didn't hear his window slide cautiously open. A gust of wind stirred the flame in the lamp chimney. The next instant a tall figure pushed one leg cautiously over the sill and slipped into the room. The intruder stood without moving a moment, his eyes gazing contemptuously down on the sleeping Barker, then snatched from the floor, where Barker had dropped it, Barker's red bandanna handkerchief. Barker's nocturnal visitor quickly knotted the handkerchief across his face to serve as a mask.

Barker stirred a trifle uneasily, then, warned by some inner sense, he abruptly opened his eyes. His jaw dropped in amazement as his mind tried to understand what was taking place. For a moment Barker thought he was dreaming. His gaze was sleep-clouded, his mind fogged with whiskey fumes. Nothing was quite clear. Everything came to Barker's mind clothed in hazy obscurity.

"Wha—what—what—?" he started to mumble thickly.

"Up on yore feet, Barker," the masked man ordered crisply, enforcing the command with a sudden tilting of the gun in his fist.

Barker staggered up from the bed, his mouth hanging dumbly open. Unbelievingly he rubbed at his bloodshot eyes.

"Never mind starin' at me," the masked man said sharply. "Turn around. Quick! I'll be pullin' trigger if you don't."

The last words penetrated Barker's dubious consciousness and he swung around with his back to his visitor. His bleary, sleep-clouded gaze had had time to note only that the masked man was clothed all in red! Something familiar about the voice though. Plainly the tones were disguised.

"Who—what is this, a hold-up?" Barker stammered.

"Right," came the short reply. "Just stand still and you won't be hurt."

The man in red lifted Barker's gun from his holster and tossed it through the open window. Then swiftly his fingers ran deftly through Barker's pockets. One by one the contents were dropped to the floor, until the masked man had found what he sought.

"That's all," came the masked man's voice a moment later. "I'll be leavin' now, Barker. But don't move until I get outside, or yo're a dead man. Understand?"

Barker nodded dumbly. He couldn't voice a

reply. His heart was pumping like mad, his knees knocking together. At his back he felt the gun-barrel removed. An instant later swift movements were heard at the open window. After that, a long silence. . . .

Still Barker was afraid to turn. After what seemed an eternity there came the sounds of horse's hoofs plunging through the rain-soaked earth. The sounds diminished rapidly.

Trembling, Barker turned cautiously toward the window. Nothing there, except the rain beating through the dark opening. Night beyond and more silence. Barker ran suddenly to the window, stopped suddenly, then peered around the edge. A trickle of water dripped from the roof to his hair. He took a long breath. The distance of a city block away, a light shone dimly from a building. Barker caught a quick glimpse of a shadowy red figure as it disappeared rapidly down the alley running at the rear of the hotel.

Barker cursed a lurid stream as he swung back into the hotel room. All traces of intoxication had been shocked out of him by this time. "Well, I'll be everlastingly damned!" he exclaimed fervently. The next five minutes were given over to a fit of vigorous cursing.

Suddenly Barker caught sight of his clasp-knife on the floor. Rapidly he stooped down and commenced to check up on his belongings. An instant later a fresh flow of profanity burst from his lips.

The bill of sale, receipting for the money he had paid John Deming, was the only object missing!

A knock sounded suddenly at his door. Barker whirled around.

"Who is it?" he snarled.

"Me—the clerk," came the answer. "What you been swearin' about. Something wrong—or are you just raisin' a drunken rumpus?"

Barker swore at the man, jerked the door open. "Drunken rumpus, eh?" he rasped. "Hell of a business! Here I been robbed—"

"Robbed!"

Barker bit his lip. Now he'd be detained. He came to a sudden decision, pointed to the open window. "The bandit came in there, while I was asleep. You skin out and get Deputy Collier. I'll go up and wake Tonto and Higgins. They might have heard somethin'—"

"Did the robber get much?" the clerk asked dumbly.

"All the money I had," Barker lied. "Dammit! What you standin' there for? Go get the deputy. Tell him to come on the run—unless the sheriff is back by this time—"

"Sheriff's still out of town. On the trail of that feller that stuck up the stage two weeks back—"

"Dammit! I know why he left town. He might as well be back. He'll never get that feller. You goin' to stand there all night? Go get Collier."

The clerk vanished before the torrent of

profanity that accompanied the words. Growling threats, Barker made his way up to the room occupied by Tonto and Higgins. It was with considerable difficulty he awakened the pair and was let into their room. Tonto had opened the door. Higgins was sitting up, bleary-eyed, in bed.

"You two hear anything?" Barker snapped.

Tonto asked dumbly, "What do you mean—hear anything?"

Barker swore at him, then with an effort held his temper in check long enough to announce, "I been robbed."

"Robbed!" from the two in unison.

"That's what I said. Can't you get nothin' through yore heads?"

Tonto was lighting a lamp now. He looked back over one shoulder. "You didn't have much money on you, did you, Quinn?"

"I'm not thinkin' about money," Barker said testily. "He took that bill of sale."

"Huh?" from Tonto. Higgins swore suddenly and swung his legs from the bed to the floor.

"What—what we goin' to do now?" Tonto asked.

"Same as before," Barker jerked out. "We'd figured to write up another paper anyway. But I hate to lose that one Deming signed."

"But who took it?" from Higgins.

"Why could he want that?" Tonto asked.

"If I knew I'd not be standin' here tellin' you

two," Barker rasped. "I only know he was all dressed in red."

"In red!"

That started more exclamations. Barker told all he knew, which, due to his dazed condition at the time of the robbery, wasn't much.

"To make things worse," Barker concluded, "I got to get out to the ranch tonight and get that deed. The clerk downstairs heard me kickin' up a fuss. He came to see what was wrong. Like a damn fool I told him I'd been robbed. I should have thought before I spoke, but I was sort of upset. Now I got to wait until Deputy Collier gets here and tell him my story, before I can get away—"

"Ain't goin' to tell Collier about losin' that paper, are you?" Tonto asked quickly.

"Do I look like a fool?" Barker snarled.

"Nev' mind, Quinn," Higgins said soothingly, "you can take the Crooked Pass trail and save time."

Barker shivered. "Not me. I don't make a ride like that in this weather." He evaded his companions' eyes and added, "Nope, I'll take the long way around. By ridin' like hell I'll be able to make it. Once at the ranch I can get a change of horses, mebbe. I'll see when I get there."

Tonto asked slyly, "Is it just the slippery footin' that makes you want to avoid Crooked Pass, Quinn?"

Barker swore at Tonto, but didn't make direct reply. Tonto shrank back before the outburst. Higgins, in an effort to change the subject, said, "Gosh, we didn't dream you'd be here now. When Scar and me crawled into bed, we figured you'd be headin' for the Rocking-D. I 'member sayin' to Scar that you shouldn't have drank so much tonight—"

Higgins stopped short at the ugly glance his chief bent upon him. "Since *when* do I have to get your permission to do my drinkin'?" Barker growled.

Higgins didn't reply. Tonto cut in with, "Say, you don't suppose Texas would—?"

"Would what?" testily from Barker.

"I dunno," Tonto said slowly, "only, well, Texas might have come back and robbed you of—"

"And put on a red suit to do it, eh?" Barker sneered.

Tonto said doggedly, "I don't care. Figure it any way you like. I never did trust Trigger Texas very far."

Voices were heard from below. Barker said, "The clerk's back with Collier. I'm goin' down."

Barker clumped down the stairway to the lower floor to find Deputy-Sheriff Pike Collier in his room.

Collier was a lean, angular man with washed-out eyes, set too closely together, and a tobacco-dribbled chin. He was also on exceedingly friendly terms with Quinn Barker. At present he showed signs of having dressed hastily and his eyes were gummy with sleep.

"I'd a been sooner, Quinn," he commenced apologetically, "only I was in bed when this feller come after me. What's this about bein' robbed?"

"Nothin' much," Barker lied, "I shouldn't have bothered you. The feller come in the window while I was sleepin' and took a little money. I only had a few dollars on me." Barker told the story in brief detail, making no mention of the robbery of the bill of sale, however.

"Dressed in red?" Collier's eyes widened.

"That's what I said," Barker snapped impatiently. "It's a color, Pike."

"I know that," Collier mumbled, "but I don't understand. You mean he had a red suit—"

"Cripes A'mighty!" Barker said in exasperation. "I don't know for shore. I didn't get a good look at him. You're wastin' time, Pike. You better get back to the street. Question any strangers you find moving around."

"Reckon you're right, Quinn." Collier straightened up. "I'll see you in the mornin'. Goo'-night."

"Good-night!" Barker said with unwarranted emphasis.

Five minutes passed. There wasn't a sound to be heard now. All the town seemed wrapped in slumber. Ten to one Collier had returned to bed too. The rain had stopped. The moon was trying to break through a thin rift in the clouds. Quickly Barker donned his sombrero and prepared to leave. In a few moments he had slipped to the window, dropped to the muddy earth outside, already trampled by the feet of the deputy, and gained his pony's side. Once in the saddle, he moved quietly away, choosing a winding course that carried him between buildings across the alley. Once clear of the town, he swung wide to strike the trail that led to the Rocking-D, and here he jabbed savage spurs into his pony's ribs. The horse shot ahead, running recklessly along the mud-churned trail.

"I'll make it all right, barrin' accidents." Barker muttered triumphantly. Another thought entered his mind: Who was the Red Rider?

CHAPTER 9

The bright morning sun was already steaming the puddles along Gunsmoke City's main street when Jeff rode into town. Every line in Jeff's lean body bespoke weariness; deep shadows under his eyes attested a sleepless night. There weren't as yet many people abroad, though down the street, still some distance away, Jeff noted a small knot of men and horses in front of the sheriff's office. Even as his eyes fell on the group, the component members scattered toward the hitch-rack and commenced to mount.

"Somethin' up," Jeff muttered. "Wonder what's doin'?"

The riders were approaching him now. Jeff pulled his pony to a walk as the men drew near. Quinn Barker and Deputy-Sheriff Pike Collier headed the group. Behind them came Scar Tonto and Bulldog Higgins. Still farther to the rear rode Chape Stock, the lean, grizzled owner of the K-Reverse-K outfit.

With the single exception of Stock, Jeff had no use for any of the riders. Both Higgins and Tonto had been hired by Barker a year or so previous and, judging from appearances, were mighty hard characters. Jeff's chief objection to Deputy Collier was based on the fact that he and Barker were friends. Somehow Chape Stock didn't fit in with the others. Jeff had always liked Stock and knew that the man stood high in John Deming's estimation.

Jeff noticed Barker speak to the deputy. Collier looked at Jeff, then said something, low-toned, to Quinn. The riders came nearer, heading directly for Jeff. Jeff pulled his pony to a stop and sat waiting. He nodded as the men drew abreast of him.

Collier demanded abruptly, without any preliminaries, "Where in hell you been, Deming?"

Jeff's lips tightened. He didn't reply at once as his gaze ran swiftly over the group. Only in Chape Stock's eyes did he find any evidence of friendliness. The others gave him hostile glances, then looked away.

Collier reddened a trifle, reached to a hip pocket for a plug of chewing tobacco, and sunk his fangs into the brown rectangle. He masticated for a moment, then, sharply, "Did you hear what I said, Deming?"

Jeff nodded, his features bleak. "Yeah, I heard you."

"Why didn't you answer?" Collier growled. "Where you been?"

"That," Jeff replied coldly, "is none of your business so far as I can see."

An annoyed murmuring ran through the group. Collier's flush deepened. He chewed violently a moment, then spat a long brown stream. "Nice way to talk to a duly authorized representative of law and order," he grumbled.

"Well, what do you want? Get it off your chest."

Collier's reply came with brutal abruptness: "We want you to identify yore old man's body, that's what."

Jeff stiffened and went white about the lips. For a moment he couldn't speak.

Deputy Pike Collier gave a short harsh laugh. "Mebbe you wish now you hadn't been so uppity with me."

Jeff shook his head unbelievingly. "Is—is Dad—has somethin' happened to Dad—?"

Collier twisted around in his saddle, looked at Chape Stock. "You tell him, Chape," Collier said.

Stock touched spurs to his pony, pushed up to Jeff's side. He was frowning angrily at Collier and saying, "You could have broke it a mite easier to the boy, Pike." He turned to Jeff. "You see, Jeff, it's this way. I was in Puma Wells yesterday, left there early this morning. I had to come to Gunsmoke City and took the trail that leads over Crooked Pass—"

"But—but what about Dad?" Jeff asked.

"I'm gettin' to it, son. Anyway, Crooked Pass is blocked. The heavy rain yesterday and last night loosened the earth up above the pass and started a landslide. Gawd only knows how many tons of rock avalanched down that slope and into the ravine. Some of them piñon trees was swept away like they was match-sticks. It's hell, I tell you! Swept away that cabin and everythin'—plumb demolished—right down into the ravine. Trees smashed to splinters. The trail's blocked complete. I had to circle back and come in the other way—"

"But—but Dad? Was he caught in it?" Jeff tried to hold the words steady.

Stock looked away, refusing to meet Jeff's eyes. He bowed his head. "Yes, he was, Jeff. I hate to tell you, boy, but the landslide swept him right down into that ravine—off'n the pass."

Jeff shuddered at the thought of the terrible plunge to death. He started to speak, gulped heavily, and remained silent. The others were watching him with curious eyes.

Chape Stock continued, "Before I headed back to reach the other trail to town, I went down there, crawling over the rubbish, jumping from rock to rock. It was just luck that I happened to see that arm stickin' out of the wreckage. The body was well nigh covered with rock. Took me quite some spell to uncover it, then I recognized that calfskin vest of yore Dad's and—"

Jeff held up one hand for silence, holding himself with an iron will. "I'll go with you," he said in a steady voice. He wheeled his pony and swung in at Chape Stock's side. The deputy nodded and the riders continued on their way.

Jeff didn't speak until the men were well out of town, then to Stock he said, "We should have the coroner or sheriff with us, shouldn't we?"

"Coroner's on a trip up to the capital," Stock informed. "Sheriff Eaton's on the track of a hold-up man—no, I don't mean that stage robber he left to catch some spell back. He finally gave that up. Came in this morning. Then he heard about this new hold-up and left right off. I'm afeared though he won't have no luck catchin' the feller. Last night's rain shore raised hell with tracks."

"Who's been robbed?" Jeff asked, more to keep his mind from his father's death than anything else.

Stock didn't reply at once. "There's somethin' queer about it, if you ask me," he said, lowering his voice.

"How do you mean—queer?"

Stock explained, "Quinn Barker claims that some masked man, dressed in a red suit, busted into his hotel room last night and stole his money. Barker says he didn't have much cash on him—"

"Red suit?" Jeff glanced quickly at Barker, riding ahead, then turned back to Stock. "What do you mean—a red suit?"

"I'm just statin' facts." Stock shrugged his lean shoulders. "It's Barker's story, but he shore maintains that a hombre in a red suit stuck him

115

up last night. It's my personal opinion that he was lookin' through bloodshot eyes, owin' to drinkin' too much, and things just looked red. Hell, he admits he was drunk when he left the Warbonnet."

"What'd Barker do after he was robbed?"

"Sent for Deputy Collier. Then he claimed he was goin' to bed. Told Collier to get on the track of the red-suited hombre. Now here's the queer point to me. Mebbe Barker went to bed, mebbe he didn't. The fact remains that when I was ridin' into Gunsmoke this mornin', I saw Barker ridin' a short distance ahead of me. It was fairly early. When I heard he was supposed to have gone back to bed, I asked him how I happened to see him out so early this mornin'."

"What did he say?" Jeff asked.

"This is funny too, but he seemed plumb put out, like he didn't want anybody to know he'd been away. You see, he'd claimed that he just come from the hotel. Then when I told my story he seemed kind of lost for an answer. Finally he admitted he'd gone to bed all right, but only stayed there a little while."

"What did Barker do?"

"Claims that he got up, saddled his horse and went on the trail of the red-suited rider, but couldn't get no track of him. Then he come back to town and sent the sheriff on the bandit's trail. It all sort of sounds queer to me."

Jeff said, "Those clothes that Otón Madero wears are sort of a dark red."

Stock nodded. "I thought of that too."

"You seen Madero this mornin'?"

Stock shook his head, then went on, "Anyway, Barker is plumb upset about this red rider business. Him and Collier and the sheriff were more excited about that than about your—about the accident on Crooked Pass. I don't understand why Barker should take it so hard, if he didn't have much money on him—"

Jeff cut in, "You're sure it was an accident?"

"Why not?" Stock squinted quizzically at Jeff.

Jeff glanced at the riders ahead, then explained, "You see, Chape, I rode over Crooked Pass myself last night—"

"T'hell you did!" Stock looked worried. "Better not say anythin' about that—"

"Why not?"

"Can't tell how such evidence might be twisted around. When I come in with the news, first thing Barker asked me was if I found the money. When I said I hadn't seen it, that it might be covered with rock, Barker acted kind of nasty and hinted mebbe it would never be found."

Jeff looked grim. "That's exactly why I followed Dad last night. He left town carrying a heap of money. I figured to trail after him as a sort of bodyguard, without him knowin' it. The landslide hadn't happened when I rode over

Crooked Pass, and I was sure Dad was ahead of me. The only way I can figure it is that Dad was detained some place on the road, and that I passed him in the darkness—"

"You didn't catch up with him at all?" Stock asked sharply.

Jeff shook his head. "Nope. I went nearly to the Rocking-D without seein' him; then I headed off across the range to ride a spell and think things over. You've probably heard how things stand— stood with Dad and me."

Chape Stock nodded worriedly, reined his pony around a small hole in the trail, but didn't say anything.

Jeff continued, "Of course, I figured Dad must have got home—got to the Rocking-D all right, so I didn't give the matter another thought."

Stock looked queerly at Jeff but still held his tongue.

About an hour later the group of riders had reached the top of Crooked Pass, where a devastating scene of desolation met every gaze. Jeff glanced up the slope where the old cabin had stood but a few short hours previous. Now there was nothing to be seen at this point except a wide, shallow furrow denoting the passage on an avalanche of rock and tumbling boulders as the landslide had moved in its terrible rush of death and destruction. The pass was cluttered with rock and dirt and brush, but was now passable.

Jeff surveyed the wrecked slope above the pass. Deep hollows pitted the hillside, showing where mammoth boulders had rested for centuries untold. In his imagination Jeff visualized the scene of the avalanche. Possibly there had been one rock, bigger than the others, near the top of the slope that had started things. The steady rain had loosened the earth about it, throwing it off balance and starting the movement. Gradually as it rolled it had gathered impetus and loosened other boulders, and the whole had gone on and on, gathering speed as it moved, tearing and crashing down the slope to drop with a roaring crash hundreds of feet below!

Stock finally broke the silence: "We'd better leave our horses here," he suggested, dismounting. "We can climb across these rocks in the path. Farther on there's a spot where we can get down to the bottom of the ravine—where I went down before."

The others climbed down from saddles and followed Stock's lead. Scrambling, sliding, stumbling, the men worked their way to the bottom of the brush-choked, rock-strewn ravine. Now Crooked Pass was far, far above them, its ragged edge silhouetted against the sky of sapphire blue.

Once at the end of their descent, the men stopped to breathe and gaze about them. At one side, half covered with huge slabs of splintered rock and boulders, were the splintered remains of the ancient cabin. Nearby was the mangled carcass of John Deming's horse, its saddle ruined. Jeff's eyes grew moist as he recognized on one undamaged stirrup fender his father's initials J. D. studded in brass. Jeff had been present the day his father had placed those studs in the leather.

Stock led the way to the dead man's body. "It was most covered with rock when I first see it," he said, low-voiced. "Just an arm stickin' out. I managed to uncover it, but I didn't move it none. Then I rode straight for town when I see who it was. I was with John the day he bought that calfskin vest—" Stock paused, and brushed the back of one hand across his face. He went on in a firmer tone, "I wouldn't have uncovered it at all, only, well, you see, I thought there might be life left. But I saw right away, once I had moved the rocks—"

His words dwindled off into silence. A lump was swelling in Jeff's throat as he gazed at the motionless, misshapen thing that had once been a man sprawled on the earth. It lay on its left side, one shoulder and the head smashed beyond recognition. The right leg was similarly mangled and twisted grotesquely to one side. A small patch on the right knee of the overalled lifeless leg caught Jeff's eye. As though it were only five minutes ago, a picture rose in Jeff's mind—a picture of the day the elder Deming had caught his denim trouser-leg on a bit of barbed wire. Jeff remembered the argument they had had about that. Jeff had wanted his father to buy new overalls, but the elder man had stubbornly insisted on patching them himself. Arguments, always arguments, that was all there had been, it seemed, between Jeff and his father. And yet a great sorrow welled up in the boy's heart as he gazed at the mangled form.

The high-heeled riding-boots too. Those boots had been a present from Jeff. A Christmas present that produced another argument. They were of soft leather, neatly stitched with a net design. John Deming had grown angry at Jeff for buying such expensive footwear. Jeff hadn't replied to that argument. He had used his own money, and he took his satisfaction in knowing, though John Deming never admitted it, that they were his father's favorite boots.

Jeff dropped to one knee and commenced to draw from a finger on the right hand a plain gold ring that had worn thin through the years. The flesh was cold and hard to the touch. The ring came off easily.

Collier said, "Don't touch that body, Deming."

Jeff said quietly, "I'm keepin' my dad's ring. I reckon there ain't any objection to that."

"You shouldn't have done it," Collier snapped. "You could have waited until later. Better let me have that ring—"

"I'll be keepin' it," Jeff said firmly. He looked steadily at Collier. The deputy averted his eyes. Jeff thrust the ring in his pocket, then stumbled to his feet, sick at heart. He heard Collier say something about "legal identification," but the words reached him from, it seemed, far away. Blinded with tears, he stumbled away.

CHAPTER 10

Jeff was out of earshot by this time. He wandered aimlessly over the heaped piles of rock and broken branches, his mind in a turmoil. How had it happened? Suddenly he stopped short. His eyes had fallen on a cartridge-belt and holster some fifty yards from the spot where the body lay. A six-shooter was half buried in wet mud a couple of feet from the holster. Jeff stooped quickly, picked up gun and belt. They were his father's.

Quickly Jeff turned and hurried back to the group of men around the body. He didn't notice they were eyeing him strangely as he returned. No one spoke for several moments as they looked at the young cowpuncher. Jeff was too excited to notice anything unusual in the men's manner. "Look here," he exclaimed, "here's Dad's gun! He didn't have it on when he—when the accident happened. Somethin's wrong!" By this time Jeff was commencing to marshal his thoughts. "Say, Dad had a satchel with twenty-five thousand dollars—!"

"Hundred and ten thousand, you mean," Quinn Barker interrupted quickly. "Mostly in big bills. You know, Deming, at the last minute I decided to pay the whole amount—in cash. We settled the deal that way without my havin' to sign a note, or anythin'—"

"Regardless of the amount," Chape Stock put in, "the money's gone—anyway, it don't seem to be around any place. Mebbe it's buried under rock—"

"Hundred and ten thousand?" Jeff interrupted. He was commencing to get a grip on himself now. "Barker, you never saw that much money," he said quietly and with cold certainty. "There's somethin' mighty queer about this whole business. Let's look around a mite and see if we can locate that satchel—though I got a strong hunch it'll be a waste of time."

Barker glared at him. A cursory search was made, but the satchel of money wasn't uncovered. The men gathered near the body again.

Quinn Barker said, "Hell, I didn't expect to find that money anyway—"

"Meanin' you know where it is?" Jeff snapped.

"I didn't say that," Barker growled, "though I might make a guess—"

"You've said too much or too little, Barker," Jeff stated. "I'm waitin' for an explanation."

"Just a minute, Deming," Barker nodded, "we'll get to that part in good time. But there's somethin' else first: a short spell back you hinted that I hadn't paid cash, full price, for the Rocking-D. You claimed I never saw that much money. I'm goin' to prove you're plumb wrong."

"I'm waitin'," Jeff said coldly.

Barker sneered. "Seein' you don't believe I paid cash, I'll show you the bill of sale yore paw signed and the deed to the property he give me—" Barker broke off and produced the papers from his pocket, and, without releasing them, held the papers before Jeff's dubious gaze.

The bill of sale was as Barker had maintained, made out in the sum of one hundred and ten thousand dollars, witnessed by Scar Tonto and Bulldog Higgins, and signed "John Deming."

"Scar and Bulldog rode in last night, at my request, to be witnesses to the deal," Barker was saying. "I wrote out the bill of sale as dictated by yore paw, and he signed it and took my money. 'Course, I'll have to get the deed recorded in my name—"

Jeff broke in, "I'm not doubtin' Higgins's and Tonto's signatures, Barker, but I am doubtin' that the other one is Dad's—"

"What do you mean?" Barker bristled.

"Just what I said," Jeff snapped. "It looks mightily like Dad's writin', and would, doubtless, fool most folks, but it don't fool me. I'm statin', here and now, that that signature is a forgery—a clever piece of writin', I'll grant you, but a forgery nevertheless. I know Dad's handwritin' like I know my own—"

"Yo're crazy!" Barker rasped, replacing the papers in his pocket. His eyes shifted from Jeff's face as he repeated, "Yo're crazy! This business has upset you."

"Yeah," Scar Tonto put in, "an accident like this is enough to spoil a feller's jedgment. You can't blame Deming for losin' his head. He don't mean nothin', Quinn. After he's thought things over—"

Jeff refused to give up. "I'm maintainin', Barker," he snapped, "there is somethin' danged queer about this whole business. I'm callin' you a liar if you claim you paid Dad in full. The only witnesses to the deal are two of your own men. There's somethin' crooked goin' on. Where's that satchel of money? Somebody took Dad's gun and threw it over the Pass. That don't look good to me! Where's Trigger Texas? Where were you last night? By God, I want an answer to those questions."

"Far as I know," Barker replied in ugly tones, "you run Texas out of town last night. I ain't seen him since you ordered him out of the Warbonnet. Told him to git, didn't you?"

By this time Barker was firmly convinced that Trigger Texas had double-crossed him and skipped out with the satchel of money. He found some excuse for Texas in view of the fact that the man hadn't been anxious to face Jeff's gun.

"Where were you last night, Barker!" Jeff repeated.

"Me and Scar and Bulldog were all sleepin' at the hotel," Barker said promptly.

"I'll vouch for that," Deputy Collier put in, "and so will the clerk at the hotel."

Jeff gave a short scornful laugh. "Barker, you were seen ridin' in to Gunsmoke City early this mornin'."

Barker shot a quick, hateful look at Chape Stock, then said, "Well, I was in bed most of the night. The clerk can tell you that. I suppose you heard about some hombre, dressed in red, holdin' me up?"

Jeff admitted he had heard the news.

"Well," Barker continued, "I couldn't get to sleep. Toward mornin' I decided to get my horse and see if I could get on the trail of that rider in red—"

"Cripes!" Deputy Collier was wide-eyed. "I didn't know that, Quinn."

"Lot of things you don't know," Barker said shortly. "Anyway, I didn't find no trace of the bandit, so I came back to town. And you can't accuse me of takin' the money, because I didn't get out this far—even if I'd had such intentions. Hell! Deming, the hotel clerk will tell you I was at the hotel until around two this mornin' at least. He went to bed himself after that. But you can see I wouldn't have time to get out here—"

"I don't know about that part," Jeff said slowly, "but I will give you a reasonable doubt on the matter." Jeff was considering that he himself had been over Crooked Pass long before that hour, and if the hotel clerk would back up Barker's word regarding the two o'clock statement, as he undoubtedly would, that seemed to clear Barker of the matter—at least so far as committing a robbery previous to the time of the landslide. . . .

"Well," Barker sneered, cutting in on Jeff's abstractions, "you got an answer to yore questions. Now mebbe Pike Collier would like a question or so answered too."

Jeff swung around to face the deputy. "You got an opinion formed on this thing, Collier?"

Collier nodded shortly. "Where were you last night, Deming?"

Jeff replied frankly, "I followed my dad to the Rocking-D to see that nothing happened to him, if you got to know—"

"Talked to him too, I suppose," Barker said scornfully, "at the Rocking-D."

Jeff shook his head. "He didn't even know I was following him. You see, I hated to see him carryin' so much money. I was tryin' to act as a bodyguard—"

"Weren't very successful, were you?" Collier said sarcastically.

Jeff flushed. "Reckon I wasn't. But I rode nearly all the way to the Rocking-D, figurin' he was ahead of me. Finally I figured he must have made better time than I thought and arrived at the ranch. Figurin' he had got home safe, I turned around and headed off across the range. I didn't go any place in particular."

"You shore you didn't see yore paw to talk to?" Collier's tones were insulting.

"Certainly not. I didn't see him once from the time he left Gunsmoke City. I just told you that I cut off the trail, just before I got to the ranch, in the belief that Dad had arrived safely. And here's something else I'd like answered—"

"Just a minute," Collier interrupted in ugly tones. "Let me see yore gun—"

"Deming was just ridin' around the range," Bulldog Higgins was saying sarcastically in loud tones to Scar Tonto. "Just ridin' around, that's all—in the rain. It was such a bee-u-tiful night for ridin'. A pretty story I calls it."

Jeff ignored the speaker and, drawing his gun, handed it to Collier. Collier examined the cylinder, sniffed at the muzzle and then thrust the end of one little finger into the barrel. The finger came out black. "Yep," Collier announced dramatically, "this gun has been fired recent. Four of the chambers is loaded, one is empty, and—*there's one empty shell in the cylinder!*"

"You fool!" Jeff exclaimed hotly. "What's all this got to do with my father's death? His body should have been removed—" He broke off, fighting to keep his temper in control. "Certain that gun's been fired recent. I took a shot at a coyote that cut my trail last night—out on the

129

range. Missed him. I forgot to reload. As for the empty chamber—well, you know dang well most of us carry our hammers on an empty chamber. Too risky carryin' it on a loaded shell—"

"Yo're right, boy," Chape Stock cut in, "but you don't understand. If I'd realized what Collier was gettin' at, I'd have warned you. Collier ain't been square and told you what's been done. While you were walkin' around findin' yore Dad's gun, we examined the body. Collier should have told you right away. I hated to break such news, but—"

"I'll tell him now," Collier said brutally. "Deming, yore old man was dead before he was swept off Crooked Pass. Ten to one you know that, but—"

"Dead!" Jeff gasped. "Before he—?"

"Murdered!" Collier snapped.

Jeff went white. "Murdered?" He gulped heavily. "How—what—who did it, Collier? Why wasn't—?"

"Who did it?" Collier laughed sarcastically. "You don't know, of course. Well, whoever done it threw a forty-five slug into him—leastwise, we're shore it's a forty-five, judgin' from the size of the wound and the fact that you pack a gun of that calibre—"

"You accusin' me—?" Jeff commenced. He paused suddenly, realising that circumstances were working against him: he had admitted following his father; it was widely known that the

130

two had quarreled; Jeff had no one by whom he could prove that he had spent a night alone on the range; that exploded cartridge in the gun was deadly evidence; he had missed his shot at the coyote, but even that couldn't be proved. Jeff's spirits dropped as he faced the accusing eyes of the men. Only Chape Stock showed sympathy in his gaze.

"John Deming was murdered from close up," Collier was saying triumphantly. "You can see the powder burns on the clothing. The wound is under the left arm. That's why Stock didn't notice it when he first uncovered the body. Remember, old Deming was layin' on his left side. The wound didn't bleed a terrible lot. Stock didn't touch the body where it lay in the mud. Here's my deductions: the murderer took Deming's gun away, then, after grabbin' the satchel of money, shot Deming in cold blood and left him on the Pass. 'Bout the time the murderer escaped the landslide took place and swept the body down below—"

"And I'm accusin' Jeff Deming of his father's murder!" Quinn Barker snarled. "Deputy Collier, I call upon you to arrest Deming on a charge of robbery and murder. I'll swear to a warrant the minute we get back to Gunsmoke City—"

The words stopped in a sudden commotion: Jeff had leaped forward and, taking Collier by surprise, snatched his gun from the deputy's

131

grasp! Collier cursed and reached to holster for his own weapon. Jeff swung the knuckles of his gun hand. The six-shooter clattered from barrel of his forty-five, rapped Collier smartly across the deputy's grip as his mouth opened in a howl of pain.

Jeff backed away from the knot of men, his eyes on Collier. "You ain't takin' me prisoner," he grated, swinging his forty-five in a swift arc that included the others. In Jeff's mind was a firm resolve to give up his life rather than suffer arrest, charged with the murder of his father.

"Plug him, boys!" Collier squealed. "He's resisted lawful arrest. Plug him—quick!"

For a brief moment the scythe of the Grim Reaper swung perilously close to the group of angry men. Jeff was resolved to sell his life dearly as possible. Barker had moved speedily to one side. Tonto and Higgins were spreading out, moving cautiously, hands commencing to slide toward holsters. Jeff had gone into a half crouch, gun-muzzle swinging restlessly from man to man. Another second and . . .

"Don't any man pull trigger! I'm shootin' if you do!"

Barker, Collier and the two Rocking-D punchers paused abruptly, stiffened, at the words. Off to the left a few feet stood Chape Stock, six-shooter gripped in one determined fist, hammer back. The old cattleman's eyes blazed with the fire of fury. "I mean it," he barked savagely. "There's been one murder done, but there won't be a second—not while ol' Betsy Ann has a slug o' lead left in her innards. Dammit! Keep yore hands away from them irons!"

Slowly, reluctantly, Barker and his cohorts relaxed. Jeff hadn't moved. He stood as before, one thumb across the hammer of his forty-five, ready for the first antagonistic move. His face was a mask of icy resolution, his eyes were narrowed to thin slits.

Stock swore again. "You too, Jeff," he commanded. "I'm dealin' this hand. Nobody ain't goin' to fog any lead at you."

Jeff hesitated just a second, then straightened up and holstered his weapon. A long breath whistled through his tense lips.

"Stock," Collier exclaimed angrily, "what's the idea of you throwin' down on us? Yo're interferin' with the law."

Chape Stock smiled grimly. "I shore am," he admitted grimly, "but I'm savin' this boy's life too. I don't aim to stand by and see a good hombre battle against odds. Jeff might have got one or two of you fellers, but he's outnumbered. I don't figure him to be guilty of his father's murder. Alive he'll have a chance to prove his innocence. Dead, he'd be judged guilty and the matter forgotten. It strikes me that some fellers might enjoy seein' that last come to pass. I'm aimin' to prevent it, so long's I got the strength to burn powder."

"By God, I'm accusin' Deming of that murder," Barker declared.

Stock eyed Barker belligerently. "How come yo're so anxious for Jeff to swing for murder?"

"I want to see justice done—" Barker commenced.

"I'm bettin' it wouldn't be to yore likin' if it was," Stock said shortly. "I'm commencin' to do a heap of wonderin' myself as to where you got that hundred and ten thousand dollars you claim you paid to John Deming. The bank will tell us whether or not you drew out that amount—"

Barker forced a cold smile. "No, it won't. I only drew twenty-five thousand from the bank. The rest I had cached away in a safe place. I ain't trustin' all my money to no bank."

Stock said skeptically, "Had eighty-five thousand dollars cached away, did you? Huh! Nobody but a damn fool would believe a statement like that."

Barker swore an oath. "We're wastin' time talkin'. Higgins and Tonto will prove I paid that money over to John Deming and received his bill of sale for the Rocking-D. If you don't believe that, Stock, it's up to you to prove otherwise."

Stock cooled down a trifle. He knew he couldn't accept Barker's challenge to "prove otherwise." He said slowly, "I expect to help do just that one of these days. Mebbe it won't be so far off either." The old cowman turned to Jeff. "You better submit to bein' arrested, boy," he advised. "Right now, it's the safest way. You've got to have a chance to live and clear yoreself. Don't worry. You got friends in the Smoky Range country. They'll help all they can."

Jeff nodded and faced Pike Collier. "All right, deputy," he said, "I'll go with you."

"Hand over yore gun," Collier growled.

"I will," Jeff agreed, "but not to you. I'm lettin' Chape keep it for me." He quickly unbuckled his belt and handed the holstered six-shooter to Chape Stock.

"Look here," Collier protested angrily, "that gun is evidence. I got to have it. It might disappear suddenly—"

An angry snort from Stock interrupted the words.

"Are you insinuatin'," Stock roared hotly, "that I'd purposely do away with evidence, Collier, or that I ain't capable of keepin' property entrusted to my care? Why, you lousy breed of a—"

"Now, wait a minute, Chape, wait a minute," Collier pleaded, commencing to back away.

"—of a pack-mule's tick," Chape Stock went on, warming to his subject. "You measly, ornery, scab-sided, mule-eared, saddle-scarred son of a spittin' Gila Monster! Are you even hintin' that I'd do away with legal evidence? For a plugged

135

peso I'd give this gun back to Jeff and we'd all make a good fight of it. I'm sort of cravin' to kill me a coupla dung-beetles and—"

"Now, now, Chape," Collier said placatingly. "Don't get riled. I don't want any more trouble—"

"Damn rootin'-tootin' right you don't!" Stock growled.

"You can keep the gun if you feel that way about it." Collier appeared a bit shaky. "I want to do what's right."

Stock snorted. "Betcha don't know how. You'll get this gun when necessary, and it won't be tampered none either, but not until then. As I said before I'm dealin' this hand, and I'm dealin' from the top of the deck. I'll be responsible for the prisoner."

"Well, I—I—" Collier commenced a protest.

Chape Stock blew up: "Damn you from hell to breakfast, Collier, you'll do as I say. Understand that? I don't want no more talk about it. Just 'cause you wear a deputy's badge is no sign yo're any kind of a boss on this range. You try and get it through yore thick skull that yo're just a servant of the people, that's all. And you'll obey orders if you want to hold yore job much longer. Just remember that: yo're not a boss; yo're a servant—and not such a hell of a good one either!"

Collier sullenly muttered something under his breath, but with the help of the others lifted the body of the dead man. Old Stock still held his gun in his hand, and a few minutes later escorted Jeff up to Crooked Pass. Barker, Collier and the others finally gained the Pass with their lifeless burden. Jeff offered his own horse to carry the corpse, then mounted behind Stock. Slowly the riders proceeded toward Gunsmoke City.

Upon arrival in town, Jeff was at once placed in a cell by Sheriff Ike Eaton, who had returned from a fruitless search for the mysterious Red Rider. Chape Stock turned Jeff's belt and gun over to Eaton, and then left to superintend the funeral arrangements for the mangled body the men had brought back to town.

During the afternoon Gunsmoke City's coroner returned from the capital and, upon hearing the tragic news, at once empanelled a jury to hold an inquest into the killing. Testimony was given by all concerned in the affair. After being closeted a short time, the jury returned a verdict to the effect that John Deming had met death at the hands of a person or persons unknown, as the result of a gunshot. However, the jury recommended that Jeff Deming be held for trial. Jeff received a hearing before the local Justice of the Peace that night, and after pleading "not guilty" was held over, without bail being allowed, until the fall opening of the circuit court. He was at once returned to his cell. Things looked black for Jeff Deming.

CHAPTER 11

The funeral was held the following morning, and while Jeff was allowed to attend the services under a heavy guard composed of Sheriff Eaton and Deputy-Sheriff Collier, he was at once returned to his cell when the ceremony had been concluded.

In Gunsmoke City the consensus of opinion seemed to be that Jeff had first robbed and then killed his father. Folks were remembering now that the two hadn't been on friendly terms. Quinn Barker did all he could, through conversation, to keep this thought alive in the minds of the town's citizens.

Several parties went out from Gunsmoke City to search among the debris below Crooked Pass for the lost satchel of money, but without avail. Within a few days it became generally conceded that Jeff had hidden the money, and the search was relinquished.

This impression was due to a large extent to the machinations of Quinn Barker, who spent most of his time in town buying drinks for all who would listen to his conversation, the conversation pointed in such manner as to convince all to whom Barker talked that Jeff was guilty and should be tried and executed with all possible speed.

And then one evening Barker received the surprise of his life: he had returned to the Rocking-D just about supper-time in extremely good spirits. Going directly to the cook-house, where his crew was seated at supper, he found a place for himself at the long table. There were eight men seated there, in addition to Scar Tonto and Bulldog Higgins. The eight were Gabe Torango, who acted as foreman for Barker; and seven punchers known as Slab Johnson, Squint Morrell, Chuck Hastings, Frank Randall, Herb Rivers, Crooked-Nose Simpson and Pat Lagou. Torango was a big, burly individual with a loud voice. The seven punchers were an evil-visaged lot, fit hirelings for their crooked employer. John Deming had never particularly liked the looks of his crew, but when anything was mentioned concerning his thoughts to Barker, Barker had always pointed out that the work was carried out efficiently. That much John Deming had had to admit. And so, by the time the Rocking-D had changed hands, Barker had built up just the sort of crew he desired to have protecting his interests.

Barker dropped down at the long table with his men, spoke genially to the crew and then called to the cook, Greasy Dan, who was fussing over the big iron range in the kitchen. Food was placed before Barker. From time to time he chuckled softly to himself. His men could see that he was in an unusually good humor. The crew glanced at him, then directed its attention to Gabe Torango as though waiting for the foreman to speak.

"Feelin' good, eh, boss?" Torango bellowed. His words were never uttered in a normal tone of voice.

Barker drained his coffee cup, set it down, lighted a cigar. "Yo're damn right, I'm feelin' good," Barker nodded.

Torango said, "What's up?"

Barker explained. "You know, there's been a sort of rumor gatherin' around town about that Deming signature on my bill of sale. Actually there was some folks thought it was a forgery, as young Deming is claimin'. Well, I took the matter to court. This afternoon old Judge Timothy Hudson—you know he always was friendly to me—passed on the bill of sale and pronounced the signature genuine."

"What's so funny about that?" Torango asked slyly. "Ain't it genuine?"

"Certainly it is," Barker snapped hastily. "Of course it's genuine. Only I was thinkin' what a simple old fool Hudson is. All I had to do was swear that I saw Deming sign that paper. Hudson didn't even ask to see Tonto and Higgins, who were witnesses. 'Course, you want to remember that I've put one or two small cattle deals in Hudson's way, and helped him make some small profits. But he's such a trustin' old nitwit and at the same time so important to himself. Even if that signature hadn't been genuine, it would have been all the same. Hudson wouldn't have known the difference."

"As a matter of fact," Torango said loudly, "that signature ain't genuine!"

"What?" Barker's face blanched. He tried to speak, but his vocal cords seemed paralyzed with surprise. His lips moved soundlessly. Finally, "Wha—what do you mean, Gabe?"

"What I said, Quinn. You forged John Deming's signature. Yon never did give him one hundred and ten thousand dollars. All you give him was twenty-five thousand and he took yore note for the—"

"Damn you, Gabe!" Barker was on his feet now. "What do you mean by makin' a statement like that—?"

"Sit down, Quinn," Torango advised insolently. "It's time for a showdown. It won't do no good to lie to us. We know too much. To make a long story short, me and the boys are figurin' to cut in on the profits from yore little scheme. You stole the Rocking-D—don't deny it! Trigger Texas—"

An abrupt explosion of cursing interrupted the words. Barker was glaring hotly at Scar Tonto and Bulldog Higgins. "Damn you, Scar!" Barker exclaimed, "you and Bulldog have double-crossed me!"

"Easy, Quinn, easy," Tonto warned coldly. "We played you square. It was Trigger Texas that tipped over yore apple-cart and spilled things. Better let Gabe finish what he started to say, then we'll get matters settled."

Barker's face was white in the light from the swinging oil-lamps in the mess-house. "Get what matters settled?"

"It's like this, Quinn," Torango commenced in his heavy rumble. "You see, I knew Trigger Texas before he ever come to work on this range. We weren't exactly close pals, but he was friendly enough to tip me off on what you and Scar and Bulldog intended doin' here—'bout John Deming and the Rocking-D and so on. If you'd had enough sense to take us all in on yore plannin', I'd have told you that Trigger Texas wasn't to be trusted. He wouldn't keep his word to his own mother—"

Barker sneered. "Yo're runnin' off at the head, Gabe. Where do you hombres figure you got any cut comin' from my ideas?"

Torango said patiently, "We figure it that way, that's all. But gettin' back to Texas—did you really expect him to bring that money to you?"

"I ain't committin' myself on nothin'," Barker said stubbornly. "Go on with yore *habla*. I'll make my talk later."

Torango continued, "Do you suppose Texas would be fool enough to kill John Deming, get his hands on all that money, and then turn it over to you—especially in view of the fact that young

142

Deming had threatened to shoot him on sight? No, Quinn, don't accuse Scar and Bulldog of double-crossin' you. It was Texas—"

"Damn his crooked soul!" Barker said wrathfully. "I'll break his neck and fill him so full of holes—"

"Might as well save yore breath, Quinn," Torango advised dryly. "I don't reckon you'll ever set eyes on Trigger Texas again. He don't want to see you, and you won't see him neither, I'm bettin'. He's got that money. But you ain't got any kick comin'. You got the Rockin'-D—"

"But look here—" Barker commenced heatedly.

"Hold yore horses, Quinn, until I've finished," Torango interrupted. "I'm aimin' to convince you that *we'll all* go shares on this outfit—"

"Like hell you will!" Barker snarled.

Torango laughed harshly. "Before you make any rash decisions, Quinn, let me remind you that Texas dropped me a little information about how Bob Deming—Jeff's older brother—was shot—"

A burst of cursing from Barker halted the words.

Patiently Torango waited until Barker had stopped for breath, then he went on, "Yo're takin' it too hard, Quinn. Now you listen to me a minute. I knew you before you ever come to this range. You didn't know me them days over in Utah. But I remember the U. S. Mail was robbed one night. They never caught the feller that did it, but his name was—"

Barker's chair fell over with a crash as Barker backed away from the table. His gun was out now, covering Gabe Torango. "That's enough, Gabe," he rasped. "Another word out of you and I'll be pullin' trigger!"

Torango coolly shrugged his shoulders, made no effort to draw his gun. "You suit yoreself, Quinn. But killin' me won't help. I've told the boys everythin' I know about you. Think things over and you'll admit you ain't so popular in the Smoky Range country. Yo're plumb li'ble to be needin' our help. It all comes down to this—are you willin' to declare us in as pardners in the Rocking-D? Or do you want us to swing over to Jeff Deming? He'd pay well for what we could tell him."

With a trembling hand Barker reholstered his gun. A sickly smile crossed his pallid features. "All right, boys," he conceded reluctantly, "I reckon yo're all in." A second later he added, "Of course, I'd figured to take care of you anyway, when things got to runnin' right—" as he resumed his seat at the table.

"Like hell you did," Frank Randall contradicted sullenly. "We've had a taste of the way you take care of us. We helped rustle a heap of cattle off'n John Deming for you, but all we ever got was promises when you sold 'em. Meanwhile you was savin' up money—"

"Shut up, Frank," Torango roared. "That game

is done. We're dealin' from a fresh deck now. Quinn has stated we'll all be pardners. That's all we're askin'. Quinn furnishes the brains; we do the work. The Rocking-D is big enough to make us all rich. We won't have to confine our sellin' activities to our own stock either. There's plenty cows on this range—"

"We'll take care of that end of it later—" Randall commenced.

"I told you to shut up while I'm talkin'," Torango told Randall. He went on, "If you look at it some ways, Trigger Texas double-crossed us as much as he did Quinn, when he lifted that twenty-five thousand. We all should have had a slice of that. But we can afford to forget that now. Things is workin' out. We know for certain that Quinn forged Deming's signature to that bill of sale, didn't you, Quinn?"

Barker gulped, then admitted the truth of the accusation with a nervous nod of his head.

"Fine," Torango went on. "Now we're all in the same boat. Quinn won't try to double-cross us, because we make better friends than enemies. We'll do what's right by Quinn, because we'll line our own pockets playin' his game. Now let's get down to business. Is there any hitch in yore schemes, Quinn?"

Barker was so angry at the manner in which he had lost control of the situation that for a minute he refused to reply. Various ideas, plans, were coursing his mind, but, no matter how he viewed the situation, he had to admit, mentally, that his men held the whiphand. He decided to bow to the inevitable.

"Yes, there is a sort of hitch," Barker stated finally. "Jeff Deming's trial comes up in a couple of weeks. Now, there's not the least doubt in my mind but what he'll be declared guilty. On the other hand, he knows that signature is a forgery, and in spite of all we can do and Judge Hudson's ruling, he might succeed in convincin' some people that he knows what he's talkin' about. The matter is bound to come up at the trial—"

"In other words," Scar Tonto put in, "it won't do for Deming to come to trial."

"How you goin' to stop it now?" Randall demanded.

"You keep still, Frank," Torango said loudly. "The boss knows what he's doin'. I think I'm commencin' to catch the idea too."

Barker explained, "Here's my idea: I want two or three of you boys to ride into Gunsmoke City tomorrow or next day. Stay away from the Warbonnet. Instead, I want you to go to the Gay Pinto Saloon. There's always a gang of hard hombres hangin' out there, lookin' for free drinks. Mostly they're just bums, but they'll serve our purpose. Spend some money and get 'em drunk. From that point on it should be easy to get 'em worked up—sore on Jeff Deming. Put it to 'em that they owe it to the community to rid the town of such vicious characters. Once you start an idea like that, it'll surprise you how quick it gathers momentum and rolls along until—"

"Until there's a nice little necktie party, eh?" Pat Lagou grinned nastily. "It's a right idea, Quinn."

"It's an idea that's got to go through." Barker's clenched fist struck the table emphatically. "I want young Deming strung up, higher'n a kite. Once he's rubbed out, there ain't nothin' his friends can do, and things will be forgotten in short order. We wouldn't be bothered any more, see, and we'd have things our own way."

"Yore brain is workin' plumb active, chief," Torango said flatteringly. "Me, I'd never thought of that. All right, we can handle it. . . . Anythin' else you want done, or that's botherin' you?"

"Yeah, there is," Barker admitted. "It's this damn Red Rider. I'd like to know who he is and where he is, 'cause he stole that original bill of sale that John Deming gave me. That paper states that I only give him twenty-five thousand, and told the conditions of the sale—about me givin' a note for the balance and so on. Now I saw John Deming put that note in the satchel with the money. The satchel is gone."

"But it's that original bill of sale that bothers you, eh?" from Bulldog Higgins.

Barker nodded. "If that bill of sale should come

to light, it'd shore raise hell with our plans. It worries me. I been wonderin' if the Red Rider could have been Jeff Deming, and if he figures to produce that bill of sale at the trial. After I'd thought things over, it seemed reasonable to suppose that the Red Rider was young Deming."

"I don't think so," Scar Tonto put in. "We were talkin' that over before you came in, Quinn. Me'n Bulldog got it figured that Trigger Texas is the Red Rider, and the rest of the boys agree—"

Barker snorted scornfully. "Trigger Texas!"

Scar nodded. "Yes, Trigger Texas. Trigger figured to double-cross you and steal that satchel of money. He didn't want you makin' trouble for him and puttin' the law on his trail, so he comes back to town, steals that bill of sale off'n you to hold over yore head and then—"

"By Gawd!" Barker expressed sudden relief. "I believe you've hit it. So long as I don't put the law on Texas, or trail him myself, he'll leave me alone, and that paper won't turn up. . . . Still, I can't see what that red suit is for—I don't get the idea of it."

"Hell, you know how Trigger always was," Bulldog Higgins said. "He was always imaginin' himself as a play-actor, or somethin'. I remember one day Texas was readin' a magazine story about a stick-up man that dressed all in red. It was supposed to be back in the old days, in England, but Texas always did like the idea. He told me so more'n once. He was plumb enthused about the idea."

"Sounds plausible, at that," Barker nodded. "Howsomever, if the Red Rider *is* Trigger Texas, he's still hangin' around this neck of the range."

"How do you know he is?" Slab Johnson asked.

Barker paused impressively, then, "Simply this: last night the Red Rider woke up Sheriff Ike Eaton and Deputy Collier and stuck a gun under their noses. Before they was fully awake the Red Rider had drifted, plenty pronto, and taken *every gun in the sheriff's office with him.* Collier said they could hear him givin' them the laugh as he loped off down the street. The town is plenty excited about it today—"

"That was Trigger Texas, all right," Torango broke in excitedly. "As long as I've knowed Texas his biggest ambition has been to stick up a law officer. He was just pullin' a good joke before he left the country for good."

"That proves," Chuck Hastings put in, "that Jeff Deming can't be the Red Rider. Deming's in the jail—"

"Mebbe there's two Red Riders," Crooked-Nose Simpson interrupted. "Texas could be one—"

"Wait a minute," from Herb Rivers. "Have you fellers ever thought that Otón Madero might be the Red Rider? It just sort of come to me that way. He's supposed to be a bandit. Mebbe the greaser needed some extra shootin' irons for his gang. By puttin' on a red suit he could lay the blame for stealin' the guns on the Red Rider that folks been talkin' about."

Torango nodded. "Might be that way. I can imagine Madero turnin' a trick of that kind."

"It's got us all guessin' wild," Barker said, frowning. "Now, here's somethin' else to think about—today, Sheriff Eaton discovered that a tunnel had been dug under one wall of the jail buildin', said tunnel opening up in Jeff Deming's cell—"

A burst of exclamations interrupted Barker's words.

"God, he didn't escape, did he?" from Torango.

Barker shook his head. "He could have, but I reckon he's just a plain damn fool. He denied diggin' the tunnel, but wouldn't say who did. He told Eaton he wasn't goin' to run away from bein' tried for a crime he didn't do. It's a point in his favor. A lot of folks are swingin' his way now. His friends hired a lawyer for him today. You see, we got to have that necktie party."

"But who dug the tunnel?" Tonto frowned. "That more of the Red Rider's work?"

"I don't reckon so," Barker said slowly. "There's a lot of talk around town that Three-Star Hennessey and Hefty Wilkins dug it. So far, them two ain't done nothin' but grin when they're accused. Sheriff Eaton threatened to arrest 'em.

They joshed the daylights out of the sheriff, but he didn't get no place."

"Did they find a gun on Deming?" Squint Morrell asked.

Barker shook his head. "Couldn't find any evidence to even show he'd made use of the tunnel in any way. It shore made a good impression on some folks, his actin' that way. Nope, we don't dare let him come to trial."

"Look here," Torango put in, "will there be any trouble takin' Deming out of the jail when we get that necktie party started. I know Deputy Collier will do as you say, but what about Sheriff Eaton?"

Barker laughed shortly. "Eaton has been goin' straight since he was elected as sheriff, but there's somethin' in his past that won't bear close examination. Collier tipped me off. So don't worry. I've already had a talk with Eaton. He'll do as I tell him. All you got to do is get a good length of hemp that won't break and put it where it will do the most good—do *us* the most good, you understand."

Barker shifted in his chair and called to the cook, "Hey, Greasy, bring on another pot of coffee, then go out to my hoss. You'll find a couple bottles of prime bourbon to bring in. We're about to drink damnation to Jeff Deming and long life and prosperity to the Rocking-D."

"And the crew of the Rocking-D," Torango

supplemented meaningly. "The only crew in the Smoky Range country to be workin' on a profit-sharin' basis!"

Barker glared at Torango, then nodded reluctant agreement. "I know when I'm well off, boys," he admitted a trifle sheepishly.

CHAPTER 12

Chape Stock, Three-Star Hennessey and Hefty Wilkins lounged over the bar in the Warbonnet, dense gloom written plainly on their features. There were only three or four other customers in the saloon and they were down at the far end of the bar, talking to Curly. This was three days after the tunnel, leading to Jeff Deming's cell, had been discovered.

Old Stock raised his sombrero and scratched perplexedly at his iron-gray hair. "I'm dam'd if I know what we can do about the situation," he confessed reluctantly. "Now it's up to that lawyer we hired." He paused, then, "I didn't tell you before, but Lucita Madero contributed some of the money for Jeff's defence—"

"Which same is dang decent," Hefty said.

"She said it was from her and her dad both. Added to what I put in and you boys—"

"Shucks!" Three-Star frowned, "what Hefty and me gave was just a drop in the bucket—"

"By the way," Hefty asked, "where is Otón Madero hangin' out these days? I haven't seen him lately."

"Lucita says he's been in and out of town," Stock supplied the information. "I haven't seen him to talk to myself. Mostly I been tryin' to pump the Rocking-D crew when I met any of 'em in town, in the hopes that one of 'em will drop a clue some place. But none of 'em will say a word, which same proves to me that they're all in with Barker on this theft of the ranch. But how we're goin' to prove that is more than I can say."

"How we goin' to prove Jeff is innocent?" Three-Star asked moodily. "That's more important than the ranch. Dang his hide, I could almost get riled at him for not makin' a getaway after me and Hefty diggin' that tunnel. That was hard work!"

Stock nodded. "Howsomever, I'm oratin' that Jeff showed a heap of sense when he didn't grab on to that opportunity to escape through yore tunnel. If he'd run away, he never would have dared to show up in Gunsmoke City again. By escapin' he would practically have confessed to bein' guilty—in most folks' eyes. By stayin' to face trial, he's forced a lot of folks to change their minds about him."

"Just the same," Three-Star pointed out grimly, "that ain't sayin' he won't be found guilty. With all the evidence pointin' toward his doin' the killin'—"

"True enough," Stock admitted. "I'm hopin' the worst he'll get will be a life sentence. That'll give us time to dig up fresh evidence, if there's any to be dug. . . . Jeff has got the best lawyer the town affords, but on the other hand, the prosecutin' 'torney is hell for convictions and the death penalty. In addition he stands in with the judge that's goin' to try the case. I hate to admit it, boys, but I won't be surprised to see Jeff sentenced to the gallows."

"I'll be on hand to plug the hombre that pulls the rope, that's all," Hefty snapped.

"You and me both, cowboy," Three-Star nodded.

"Wish it would be Sheriff Eaton," Stock stated dourly.

"Mebbe I'll plug him anyway," Three-Star announced thoughtfully.

Hefty said, "One way or another we got to get Jeff out of this jam, somehow, if he gets the limit."

An oblong splash of morning sunlight spread across the floor, as the door of the Warbonnet was flung wide open. Lucita Madero darted inside, her gaze trying to pierce the dim interior after the brilliance of outside sunlight. She paused just inside the entrance. Stock noticed that she wore a wide-brimmed sombrero and corduroy riding skirt.

Stock stepped out from the bar. "What you doin' here, Lucita? This ain't no place for a girl!" Hefty and Three-Star whirled around, giving vent to exclamations of astonishment as their eyes fell on the girl.

Lucita stepped quickly into the room. Her face

155

was pale. "*Madre de Dios*!" she burst out. "I hoped to find one of you here. Father was going for a ride with me this morning. I'd promised to get the horses at the livery. I saw—"

"Look here, Lucita," Three-Star commenced, "you can't stay in here. If anythin's wrong, we'll talk it over outside—"

"Enough, Three-Star," the girl interrupted impatiently. "I know what I'm doing. Come, hurry! There is a mob gathering about the jail. I heard threats of lynching Jeff. It's a bad crowd— you know those plug-uglies that hang out at the Gay Pinto—"

"Sufferin' rattlers' puppies!" Hefty growled. "I'll bet Barker is behind this—"

"Oh, come quickly," Lucita pleaded. "We're wasting time!" Words tumbled excitedly from her lips.

Hefty and Three-Star had already leaped outside, heading for their ponies at the hitch-rack. The girl whirled to follow them. Chape Stock swung back to the bar, ignoring the excited questions of Curly and the other customers.

"Quick, Curly," Stock barked, "lemme have that scatter-gun of yours."

Brushing aside the words of the customers who hadn't caught the import of Lucita's words, Stock seized the double-barrelled shotgun Curly handed up from beneath the bar and dashed for the roadway!

As Stock reached the door he saw that Hefty and Three-Star were already in saddles. "I'm on yore heels, boys," he shouted. "Shoot first and talk later!" A short distance behind the two cowboys, Stock saw Lucita gaining her pony's back, even as she swung the nimble-footed beast away from the tie-rail. The horse pivoted on hind hoofs as the girl settled to the saddle. Then she dug in spurs and the pony leaped ahead.

"Damn the luck!" Stock swore. "This ain't no business for a girl—"

The words ended in a sudden grunt as his grizzled form collided with that of Otón Madero who was just about to enter the Warbonnet. Both men staggered back from the impact.

Madero recovered first, laughing, "Ten thousand pardons, Señor Stock. It was my fault."

"Nev' mind that," Stock panted. "There's a lynchin' party started—goin' to hang Jeff Deming! Lucita heard them talkin' on their way to the jail. She come here to get us—"

"So?" Madero broke in swiftly. "I will go with you. There is my caballo at the hitch-rack where Lucita left him. Come!"

The two men dashed out to their ponies, Stock vaulting into the saddle, carrying Curly's shotgun, with an agility surprising in one of his years. "C'mon," he snapped. "Jeff is goin' to need every friend he's got!"

But Madero was already under way. He and

Stock were tearing along the street at breakneck speed. Hefty, Three-Star and Lucita weren't more than a hundred yards ahead of them.

Stock cursed and yelled to Madero, "Better get hold of yore datter and keep her out of this!"

Madero nodded comprehension, called back through the rush of wind, "My 'Cita, she knows how to take care of herself."

"I shore hope so," Stock muttered, urging his pony to greater efforts.

From the corner of his eye as the riders flashed along, Stock glimpsed a swiftly unrolling panorama of street, excited men, running figures and plunging horses. He drove cruel spurs into his pony and grunted with satisfaction on noting that Madero was keeping even with his best efforts.

"Bandit or not," was the thought that coursed through Stock's mind, "this Madero hombre is a man!"

He could hear the yelling and hooting of many men now. As his horse carried him swiftly along the uneven, rutted thoroughfare, the noises became more distinct. Stock swung his pony around a long curve in the street, almost sweeping the sure-footed little animal off its hoofs, as he leaned far over. The next instant the jail flashed into sight.

Stock got the whole picture in a brief glance. Standing on the front step leading to the jail entrance—the jail was a square, squat building of adobe and iron-barred windows—were Sheriff Eaton and Deputy Pike Collier, pretending to dissuade from its purpose the horde of drunken, swearing, yelling men clustered about the building, many of them carrying hempen ropes.

There were probably fifty men in the crowd—renegade whites, half-breeds, down-at-the-heel cowpunchers, tinhorn gamblers and plain, everyday bums. Eyes intent on the jail, the yelling horde wasn't aware of the riders coming swiftly at its rear.

The mob scattered suddenly as Hefty and Three-Star, with Lucita at their heels, rode straight into it. A man went sprawling on one shoulder. A few who had started to run now returned upon seeing they had only two punchers and a girl to contend with. Again they closed in.

Hefty and Three-Star backed their ponies to the jail entrance and, guns in hands, ordered the would-be lynchers to disperse. A moment later, Lucita joined them at one side, having jerked out her own six-shooter by this time, the smaller calibre weapon looking mighty deadly in her determined grip.

A loud hooting rose on the air. Hefty's and Three-Star's words were drowned in an angry roar of abusive defiance:

"Get out or get killed!"

"Tell that woman to get away from here!"

"It's her own fault if she gets hurt!"

"C'mon, boys, get yore ropes ready!"

"String Deming up!"

Someone hurled a rock through the air. It missed Hefty by inches and landed with a heavy crash against the jail door. The door swung open slightly. Under the circumstances, it should have been locked. Collier and Eaton stood to one side, getting ready to save their own skins from flying missiles. Three-Star yelled something at Eaton, but the sheriff replied only with a helpless gesture of his hands.

As Chape Stock and Madero drew near, they saw Herb Rivers, Pat Lagou and Slab Johnson hovering about the rim of the crowd, urging the men on. With Madero at his heels, Stock headed his pony directly to the centre of the densely packed gang!

Spurring, the two riders drove in and in. Again men scattered in all directions, but at Slab Johnson's shouted commands, quickly gathered and returned to the assault. The mob closed in. All around Stock and Madero was a writhing ring of hate-contorted faces, snarling mouths, bloodshot eyes. The drunken cursing swelled to a maniacal beast-like roaring.

With hands clutching at clothing, stirrups and bridles, Stock and Madero fought their way to places on either side of Hefty, Three-Star and the girl. Madero shouted something at his daughter, but the white-faced Lucita refused to leave, shaking her head.

Stock bawled out: "Scatter, you measly scum of border lice! Back up, before I puncture yore lousy, stinkin' hides!"

His orders were supplemented by similar orders from Madero, Hefty and Three-Star. Stock shifted momentarily in the saddle, spoke, low-voiced, to Eaton and Collier standing motionless at his horse's tail, "Damn you, Eaton," Stock snapped, "Show some authority. Break this mob up!"

"I done the best I know how, but they're too strong for me," Eaton protested tremblingly. "I—I asked 'em not to make no trouble—"

"Asked 'em, my aunt!" Stock bawled indignantly. "This ain't no time for askin'! Get yore guns into sight. You ain't even drawed hardware yet, you crooked, cowardly snakes—"

A flying beer bottle, intended for Stock's head, missed its mark and took Eaton squarely between the eyes. The sheriff went down like a poled ox, then staggered to his feet just as Hefty released a slug at the man who had thrown the missile! There came a sharp yelp of pain and the mob commenced to back away. "Stick to 'em, men!" Slab Johnson roared angrily. "There's only four of 'em and a woman. You ain't afraid of no woman, are you? Watch me!"

His six-shooter came flashing out, cutting a brilliant arc in the bright sunlight. Madero's gun-hand moved slightly . . . unleashed a stinging stream of fire and smoke from his six-shooter barrel! Johnson's arms flew into the air and he pitched down under the booted feet of the mob! It hesitated, then again, angrily, pushed forward!

A bullet *whupped* into the adobe wall, back of Three-Star. Another cut through the brim of his wide felt hat. The cowboy laughed grimly and commenced thumbing his gun. Two more of the would-be lynchers crashed down.

A leaden slug whined off the saddle-horn in front of Chape Stock. He emptied his Colt gun; then, seeing that stronger medicine was necessary, he lifted Curly's shotgun and sprayed the foremost figures with a scathing shower of buckshot. Men went to their knees, staggered forward, sagged limply—falling in all directions!

It was the shotgun that did the work. The mob wavered, broke, and retreated, and in its foremost ranks were Herb Rivers and Pat Lagou. As the cowardly gang fled down the street, Stock and his companions sent slug after slug screaming at its heels.

Madero turned and looked at Lucita. The girl was white, her red lips quivered a little, but her chin was up, determined. She had started to push her gun back into its holster.

"I think that is all, my 'Cita," Madero said softly.

"I—I—" Lucita gulped, "I didn't even shoot once. Golly, Dad, I was frightened."

Madero laughed. "So were we all, my little one. I think it best for you to return to your shop now."

Lucita nodded. Without speaking she waved one hand at the others and turned her horse, heading along the street toward her place of business.

CHAPTER 13

Sudden quiet had descended on the street. The dust settled back. The only indications left of the fight were found in the huddled, groaning figures sprawled in the roadway. A few lay silent, without movement. Peaceful pedestrians commenced to put in an appearance. A crowd gathered slowly about the jail, but the intentions of this crowd were peaceful, based only on curiosity. Somebody sent up a call for a doctor. Two or three of the injured managed to rise and hobbled hastily from the scene.

Stock was gazing down the street after Lucita's vanishing figure. "There's a girl with spunk," he announced. "I'm glad to see her leave when she did, though. There's goin' to be a mess to clean up here."

The others nodded. Hefty said, "A woman's nervy in some cases."

Stock produced a chunk of Grangers' Twist, bit off a generous mouthful, chewed a moment, shifted it from jaw to jaw, and remarked laconically, "Well, we druv 'em off, boys."

"We certain did," Three-Star said grimly.

Madero smiled, "They were rats, no? Cowardly rats!"

"The name's too good for 'em," Stock growled.

164

He slung the empty shotgun across his knees and commenced to punch out the exploded shells in his six-shooter. He reloaded without haste, then shifted his weight around to face Sheriff Eaton and Deputy Collier who were standing silently by.

"You two," Stock stated contemptuously, "are the *worst* rats! Eaton, you'd never have got into office if folks had knowed what their vote was goin' to bring 'em. And yore deputy is just as bad. Yo're just a couple of cowardly, stinkin', four-flushin', double-crossin' buzzards, that's what you are!"

Pike Collier swore. "I ain't takin' that from no man," he snarled, dropping back a pace, one hand reaching to gun-butt.

Stock spat a long brown stream that splashed on Collier's boots, and eyed the belligerent figure gravely. "Ain't you, now?" he said quietly. "Why don't you jerk yore iron then? I'm waitin'." He masticated calmly a few moments, but his eyes were narrowed to thin slits of angry fire as he waited for Collier to back up the words that he had uttered. Again Stock spat scornfully.

Collier backed away a step, releasing hold of his gun-butt. "We'll settle this some other time, Stock. You got too many friends with you now. 'Sides, I got duties, There's wounded out there," gesturing to the street.

"Get to yore duties," Stock said contemptuously.

Collier hastily stepped to the street and stooped at the side of Slab Johnson who lay sprawling and groaning in the dust.

Sheriff Ike Eaton had been trying to nerve himself to face Stock. Now the sheriff said in blustering tones, "Now, you look here, Stock, you've talked in a mighty high-handed manner. I ain't goin' to have—"

"You cravin' a battle, Eaton?" Hefty snapped hotly.

"I certainly ain't," Eaton said hastily. "Me, I aim to enforce the law—not break it."

Three-Star grinned sarcastically, chuckled, "Pike and Ike, they're just alike. Both of 'em yeller dawgs!"

"That's not true," Eaton said weakly. He gathered his last remnants of courage and changed the subject slightly, "Stock, I'm afraid I'll have to arrest you fellers for startin' this shootin'—"

"We'll make you *afraid* if you try it," Stock barked savagely. "Arrest us for preventin' a lynchin', eh? Why, damn yore hide, Eaton, yo're lower than I thought. I got a good notion to plug you right here and now and rid Gunsmoke City of a stinkin' cur. You just try to arrest us and see how far you get with that idea. What you better do is get them bodies cleaned out of the roadway—either get 'em to a doctor or to the undertaker's. Any wounded that recovers

166

you'd better run out of town. Now get busy!"

"Ye—yes, I reckon yo're right, Chape," Eaton faltered. "I'll do as you say. And I reckon we won't say anythin' more about arrestin' you boys. I kind of misspoke myself in the excitement."

"You shore did," Stock growled. "While you and Collier is cleanin' up the mess, me'n my friends will go in and visit Jeff. Gimme yore jail keys."

"Hell, Stock, I can't turn my keys over to you—"

"Gimme them keys!" Stock roared angrily. Eaton jumped as though he had been shot, then meekly handed over the keys. "I'll give 'em back when we're through visitin'," Stock went on. "And don't be afeared I'll let yore prisoner escape. I won't."

Followed by Madero and the two cowboys, Stock dismounted and pushed open the front door of the jail. Passing through the small office that fronted the cells, where sat a white-faced, spineless individual who was supposed to function as the jailer, Stock made his way to Jeff's cell. Here the iron-barred door was quickly unlocked and the men stepped inside. Jeff greeted them with a smile.

"Sounded like there was a mite of excitement outside," Jeff said. "Judgin' from certain remarks I heard, some hombre had me framed for a necktie party that might have come off, except for the arrival of you fellows. That dang jailer out there was afraid to go outside, and he refused to do anythin' to protect me. I wanted him to get me a gun, so I could protect myself, but of course he wouldn't. Anyway, I'm sure obliged to you hombres—"

"What the hell!" Three-Star exclaimed suddenly. "What they got you handcuffed for, Jeff?"

Jeff glanced down at the steel bracelets that encircled his wrists, shrugged his shoulders. "You got me. Eaton insisted on puttin' 'em on this mornin'."

Chape Stock swore a lusty oath, ending, "It goes to prove that Eaton knew a lynchin' was supposed to come off. He hobbled you to make things easier for the mob when they broke in. Lucky I got his keys. We'll have 'em off in a minute."

While the keys were being sorted and the cuffs removed by Stock, Madero and the two cowboys were telling Jeff about the attempted lynching.

". . . and it was Lucita that brought us word," Three-Star was saying. "The girl broke in on us at the Warbonnet—"

". . . rode hell for breakfast with us," enthusiastically from Hefty. "Backed her horse up against the jail and faced that mob. Her gun was out—"

"My 'Cita is not lacking in the bravery," Madero stated proudly.

"Gosh," from Jeff, "I hate to see her running risks like that."

The cuffs were removed now. Jeff rubbed his wrists, flexed his muscles.

"If the Señor Jeff wishes to make the escape," Madero proposed gravely, "perhaps I could help." He glanced quickly out at the other cells which, at present, were empty, and went on, "I have my men—certain friends—who will be pleased to help. We could over-power the jailer, tonight, and give you time to make—what do you call it?— the getaway? *Si*, the getaway."

Jeff smiled, shook his head. "Much obliged, Señor Madero, but I don't reckon we'd better do it that way. That would get you in wrong. People would be sure to suspect. Howsomever, before this affair is settled, I may need help from *all* of you."

The others nodded. The men talked for a few minutes longer. Finally, Stock suggested leaving. "We better be driftin'. We'll drop in on Lucita and let her know that everythin' is all right with Jeff. . . . S'long, boy. Keep a stiff upper lip. We'll be droppin' in to see you again, soon."

A few moments later, having relocked Jeff's cell door, the four men stepped into the street. Pike Collier was nowhere in sight, nor was the craven jailer who had been seated in the small room in front of the cells when the men entered.

Standing before the jail, gloomily chewing on

169

a matchstick, stood Sheriff Ike Eaton. He averted his eyes as Stock and the others stepped into the open air.

Stock said shortly, handing the ring to the sheriff, "Here's yore keys, Eaton. And don't ever let me hear of you handcuffin' Jeff Deming again. It don't look square. 'Nother thing, if you don't get on the job and 'tend to things better, yo're shore goin' to have to explain things to me, personal—and you'll be lookin' down the bar'l of ol' Betsy Ann when you do it—"

"I—I will—shore, I will, Mister Stock," Eaton stuttered eagerly. "I don't want no trouble with you. I already started an improvement. I—I fired that jailer we had. He wa'n't no good. Pike Collier will be takin' care of his job from now on. Pike's goin' to move his cot right down to the jail and make shore there ain't no more lynchin' attempted—"

"Phaugh!" Stock spat disgustedly. "That ain't no better. Pike ain't to be trusted. To be frank with you, Eaton, I'm expectin' more trouble. Just because one hemp party fell through ain't no sign another won't be attempted. Now, since you've made Collier the jailer, I'm aimin' to take even more interest in this affair. . . . Eaton, you've fell down on yore job bad. If I was you, I'd resign plumb pronto and get out of town. I'll give you a word of warnin': look out for me if anythin' happens to Jeff Deming—savvy?"

Eaton nodded dumbly, his brow furrowed with worried lines. While he was trying to frame an appropriate answer—one that would uphold the dignity of his office—Stock, Madero and the two cowboys mounted their ponies and trotted off down the street.

Eaton drew a long breath when Jeff's four friends had disappeared. "Whew!" he muttered nervously. "Now I am in a tight. If anythin' happens to young Deming, I got to face Stock. And if certain things don't happen to him, I'll find myself lookin' into Barker's gun muzzle. My Gawd! What'll I do? I reckon Barker would be the worst—but it might be a toss-up. I'd shore hate to get old Stock riled much more than he is. What'll I do? Reckon it might be a good idea for me to leave town for a spell and let Pike Collier run this job in my place. Nope, I can't do that. As a legally elected sheriff of the county, I got to stay here and face what's comin'. And I don't like the look of things a-tall."

CHAPTER 14

Three events of considerable importance occurred that night.

Deputy-Sheriff Pike Collier played a prominent part in one of the happenings, but it took place so quickly and with such efficient dispatch that he was able to explain only vaguely just what had happened.

Collier, in his position as jailer, had been awakened from his cot, at the front of the jail, by the sound of Jeff's voice. Jeff was calling for a drink of water. Grumblingly, his eyes heavy with sleep, Collier had procured a tin cup of water and shuffled back to Jeff's cell. That day, after Stock and Jeff's other friends had departed, Collier had taken special pains to ascertain that no weapons had been left with the young cowboy. However . . .

Collier didn't carry a light as he moved back to the cell with the cup of water. Enough starlight showed through the outer window of Jeff's cell to show the form of the young cowboy silhouetted against the barred door. The deputy had just passed the cup of water through the iron bars when he felt the cold muzzle of a Colt gun jammed, with no little force, against his ribs. At the same instant, Jeff's left hand dropped the cup and, passing through the bars, seized Collier by the throat.

"Open the door, Collier!" Jeff's tones had been hard, grim, commanding. At the words, Collier gurgled something unintelligible and tried to shrink away from the gun. Jeff pulled him closer, prodding him with the Colt barrel.

Collier choked. Jeff released his hold a trifle. Collier stammered something about not having the keys to the cell.

"Don't lie, Collier," Jeff said sternly. "I heard you tell Eaton you'd keep 'em in your pocket. Your pants are on. Come on, produce those keys pronto—either that or I'll—"

Collier didn't argue the matter longer. He produced the keys and opened the cell door. Jeff stepped into the corridor, swinging the door back before his advance, in an effort to sweep Collier out of the way. As he released his hold on the man's throat, Collier darted around the edge of the door and closed with Jeff. Jeff hit him once. Collier, gamely, struck back. Not wishing to lose time, Jeff raised his six-shooter and brought the heavy barrel sharply down on Collier's head. Collier grunted once and slumped to the floor, unconscious.

Moving like a wraith in the darkness of the corridor, Jeff quickly stepped over the body of the deputy jailer and hastened toward the outer doorway. Once in the open air, darkness swallowed his lithe movements as he darted around to the back of the jail.

Sometime that same night, while the proprietor of the Blue Front Livery was over to the Warbonnet Saloon getting a drink, someone entered the stable and stole Jeff's horse, saddle and bridle. The theft wasn't discovered until some hours later—if theft it may be called.

The night seemed fraught with mysterious happenings, one of which occurred in the sheriff's office, located some short distance from the jail. Here Eaton slept, in addition to employing the office for the discharge of his legal duties.

For the second time in his life, Sheriff Ike Eaton was awakened from a sound sleep by the Red Rider. This time the Red Rider did more than just take all the guns in the sheriff's office. He ordered Eaton to leave town immediately, enforcing the command with an unwavering muzzle of a six-shooter. Eaton, after one scared glance into the cold, relentless eyes showing through the mask of the Red Rider, decided to obey with all the haste at his command. The following morning the sheriff's abrupt resignation, written in a trembling hand, and *witnessed by the Red Rider,* was found on the desk in the office. Eaton was never again seen in Gunsmoke City.

The resignation wasn't discovered until broad daylight. Meanwhile, Deputy Collier was recovering consciousness and picking himself from the jail floor. He staggered around in the dark for a time then, on shaky legs, headed for the reviving freshness of the open air.

Collier never knew how long he had been unconscious. He may have been "out" an hour. On the other hand, perhaps only a minute had elapsed. Collier couldn't say with any degree of certainty. Of one thing he was sure, however: when he rose to his feet and staggered to the doorway for air, he was just in time to see a masked figure in red clothing loping past the jail, along the darkened street.

A good many folks claimed this was all Collier's imagination when the news broke the next day, but nevertheless, within a few hours, Gunsmoke City was rife with rumors as to the motives of the Red Rider—but they were only rumors.

But the question that occupied the greatest number of minds was: who is the Red Rider?

CHAPTER 15

Three nights after Jeff's escape from jail, a trio of men were seated about a small greasewood fire in a tiny ravine located in the heart of the Trozar Mountains. One of the men was Jeff Deming; the other two were Three-Star Hennessey and Hefty Wilkins.

The small fire blazed with considerable sputtering and reflected its flickering lights on the intent faces of the three and on the dust laden leaves of the brush thicket at their backs, where the horses were picketed. Three-Star plucked a crackling twig from the fire and touched it to the brown paper cigarette between his lips, then tossed the twig back in the dancing blaze.

"Of course I'm with you, Jeff," he laughed. "Didn't expect anythin' else, did you? I know Hefty will throw in with you, too. Ordinarily, I hate to see a good hombre turn to rustlin', and ordinarily, I hate a cow-thief worse'n poison, but these is extenuatin' circumstances, as you might say."

"Extendin' what?" Hefty frowned. "Where'd you get that word?"

"The question is," Three-Star interpreted, "are you throwin' in with Jeff's plan, or ain't you? Can you understand that much?"

"Certain I'm throwin' in with Jeff," Hefty growled. "I'm with him from hell to breakfast. Didn't think you'd need to ask."

"That's fine," Jeff nodded gravely. "I thought you'd both trail along with me, but I wanted you both to consider the risks as well as the profits—"

"We're considerin' the fun," Hefty smiled. " 'Course, while Three-Star won't admit it, he's an old hand at pickin' up stock that don't belong to him—"

"Yo're a blasted per—per—pervirkator—" Three-Star stumbled over the word.

Hefty smiled contemptuously. "It's a cinch you can't explain that one, Three-Star. Hereafter, you better confine yore learnin' of new words to what you can read off'n tomato cans and such. Now, shut up. I want to hear what Jeff's said. We've both announced that we hate rustlers and we've both agreed to throw in with Jeff on a job of stock stealin'. All right, Jeff, go ahead."

Jeff nodded. "I'm against rustlin' myself, as you know. But this is different. I'm certain in my mind that Barker forged Dad's signature on that paper. I can't prove it, but I *know* it just the same, in my heart. In the second place, I figure what money he might have paid to Dad he got stealin' Rocking-D cows. So that money wasn't rightfully his, but Dad's."

"We're agreed on that," Hefty nodded. "Quinn Barker is a skunk of the first water."

"That bein' the case," Jeff continued, "I'm goin' to start pickin' up all the Rocking-D cows I can lay my hands on. We three will split the profits—and the risks. Once we get some money, mebbe I can do a little investigatin' and learn exactly who killed Dad—"

"Barker was back of that," and Hefty swore a bitter oath.

"Of course," Jeff agreed, "but I want to get proof, just as I want to get proof as to who killed my brother, Bob. But we'll get some Rocking-D stock and sell it first—"

"Chape Stock goin' to throw in with us?" Hefty asked.

Jeff shook his head. "I didn't even mention the subject to Chape, and don't intend to. He's a good friend of mine. Besides, he's got his own K-Reverse-K outfit to think of. Consequently, he'd have more to lose, if something went wrong with my plans. I don't aim to get Chape into trouble. He's too old a man to start bucking the law now, and you know what'll happen if we get caught."

Three-Star affected a mock shudder, then grinned. "Let's not mention that subject. . . . Jeff, have you thought out a way to dispose of any cattle we pick up?"

Jeff nodded promptly. "I had somethin' like this planned in my mind, even before I escaped from the jail," he explained. "The night I made my getaway, I met Otón Madero just outside the town limits, and told him what had happened. We had a long talk and got several things settled before I asked him to get word to you two boys to meet me here. To cut a long story short, Madero will take the cows off our hands. All we've got to do is run them over the Border line, and from then on, Madero will dispose of them and pay us the proceeds. You see, Madero has the crew to handle things, from all he tells me."

Hefty said slowly, "The plan sounds airtight. Folks mebbe wouldn't approve of it, but, Jeff, I think yo're doin' the right thing."

Three-Star changed the subject: "What I want to know," he said, "is where you got that gun to escape with, that night."

Jeff didn't reply for a minute, then, "I can't tell you much about that, because I don't quite understand it myself. All I know is that someone came to my outside cell-window, dropped my belt and gun through the bars and whispered that my horse was waitin' around back of the jail, saddled and ready to go. Whoever it was, disguised his voice, sounded like. After that attempted lynchin', I'd decided I'd better not stay and wait for trial."

"You wouldn't get a square show anyway," Hefty said bitterly. "Not with Quinn Barker runnin' things the way he is."

"It must have been the Red Rider give you yore

gun and got yore horse from the livery," Three-Star offered. "It was him stuck up the sheriff's office, a spell back, and cleaned out all the weapons. Yore gun was among 'em, bein' held as evidence. Then, the night you escaped, it was the Red Rider that run Sheriff Eaton out of town."

Jeff smiled. "You don't mean to say that Eaton has left town?"

Three-Star looked queerly at Jeff. Hefty frowned. Three-Star finally nodded, saying, "They found Eaton's resignation on his desk, the morning after you escaped. It read that he was takin' the Red Rider's advice and movin' on. The Red Rider witnessed the sheriff's signature—just 'Red Rider,' of course—no real name signed. Deputy Collier is takin' his place. That's all we know, except that folks is doin' a heap of guessin' as to the Red Rider's identity."

Hefty hesitated a moment then asked awkwardly, "Uh . . . er . . . say, Jeff, you ain't the Red Rider, are you?"

Jeff grinned his amusement. "What makes you think that, Hefty?"

"There's a heap of folks think you are," Three-Star supplemented, before Hefty could reply. "You see, they figure you might have been the one that stuck up Quinn Barker that night at the hotel. Then, after that tunnel to yore cell was discovered, they got to thinkin' you might have held up the sheriff's office and made off with his guns—includin' yore own what was bein' held for evidence. You know, you could have done it, and then slipped back into yore cell, 'thout yore absence bein' noticed. So that's why—"

"Yeah, I could have," Jeff answered rather absent-mindedly, "but, shucks, you don't want to believe everythin' you hear. There's more important things to think of, if we intend to turn rustlers. Let's get our broncs."

Hefty and Three-Star looked their surprise. "You figurin' we should get started to-night?" Hefty queried.

"Exactly," from Jeff. "Madero and his men will be waitin' for us about dawn, at the Mexican end of Cayuga Canyon, just over the line. I've been spyin' out the range and, for this first job, I aim to hit Barker where it will hurt worst: over near Cottonwood Mesa, Barker's holdin' a special bunch of about a hundred-fifty white faces. They're prime stock that he's fattenin' for a special market. We'll get those first. C'mon."

He rose to his feet and the two cowboys noted that his holster was tied firmly to his right thigh with a strip of rawhide. Jeff, noting their curious glances, said, "Yeah, there might be a mite of lead-slingin'. Barker has got Squint Morrell, Frank Randall and Crooked-Nose Simpson ridin' herd on the cattle. Those three were all I saw when I was spyin' out the lay of the land, though Barker might send out additional riders for night duty. We'll have to chance that. . . . I've been watchin' 'em from a rise of ground with my field-glasses. After to-night we'll figure to run off unguarded stock, but I want to give Barker somethin' to worry about, first off."

The spot at which Quinn Barker was holding the particular herd which Jeff planned to run off was less than ten miles from the Mexican border. This, of course, was a point advantageous to Jeff's plans. It was shortly after midnight when Jeff and his two companions first spied the light of the fire indicating the presence of the Barker forces. Jeff and his two companions immediately pulled their ponies to a walk.

The moon was high in the heavens now, touched only now and then by drifting wisps of cloud-shapes. Jeff realised it would be little use trying to approach unseen. From a distance he could see the cattle bedded down, some two hundred yards from the campfire. To his ears came the voice of the nighthawk, raised in a song that was supposed to keep the steers quiet:

Coffee an' beans an' a ten-dollar hoss-s-s
Is the best I get from my tight-wad
    boss-s-s;
I break a hoss, then the hosses break me—
A-drivin' these critters for the Rockin'-D!

Our grub is beans without no pie,
Our coffee's just like ink-k;
The water's so full of alkali-i-i
That you can't hardly drink-k-k!

The Rockin'-D is a dang fine spread
To earn yore wages an' sourdough bread.
But I'm cravin' my home in Okmulgee
Where a man lives on 'baccy an' good
    whis-kee-e-e!

"Fine voice," said Three-Star with a shudder. "Did you ever hear anythin' so sour?"

Hefty nodded. "Sounds like somebody tearin' a rag. I swear if I was a cow critter I'd roll my tail at the first note. Sounds like Pat Lagou's caterwaulin'. Must be more than three men with the herd."

"Probably is," Jeff agreed. "Three men at the fire—two ridin' herd. Tie your bandannas across your faces. They'll serve as masks." He was already drawing up his own neckerchief across his nose.

The other two followed suit. "Any particular plan?" Hefty asked.

Jeff said, "We'll ride straight to the fire, get the drop on the three hombres sittin' there and tie 'em up. They won't be expectin' trouble, so it should be easy."

"How about the two hombres ridin' herd?" Three-Star wanted to know.

"We'll have to see what they do first," Jeff said quietly. "Mebbe they won't notice anythin' wrong at the fire, then we can get the drop on them later. They might decide to make a run for it, if they do notice anythin' wrong. But I'd like the whole business to be carried off as smooth as possible. Don't throw lead unless they start it. . . . C'mon!"

The three put spurs to their ponies and broke into a lope that rapidly closed the distance between horses and the campfire ahead.

As Jeff and his companions neared the fire, they saw three shadowy figures silhouetted against the leaping flames. These three had gained their feet and stepped forward a few paces to learn who was approaching. By this time the singing near the herd had stopped.

Glancing across the intervening yards that separated steers from the camp, Jeff sighted two riders. He lifted his voice slightly to reach his companions: "They got five men, all right. Barker must be expectin' trouble; either that or he's so crooked he just don't trust nobody—"

At that moment a hail reached Jeff and his friends from the camp: "Who are you and what do you want?" came Crooked-Nose Simpson's hoarse tones.

Jeff didn't answer. He spoke swiftly, low-voiced, to Hefty and Three-Star. "Don't pay any attention. Keep goin'. We'll be on top of 'em in another minute. We'll talk then—"

Abruptly, a crimson tongue of flame pierced the night. Jeff felt the breeze of a thirty-thirty slug as it whined viciously past his body. Instantly, he reached to six-shooter, thumbed a swift shot in reply.

A second shot screamed through the night, coming from the camp, then a third. However, Jeff and his companions were moving too fast now to make good targets. The two riders near the herd paused uncertainly for a moment, then decided to come in to the fire.

Straight into a veritable hail of whining lead Jeff rode, lances of flame and smoke spurting from his right hand. One of the men near the fire spun half around and plunged on his face! A second stumbled to his knees, raised one arm for a last, futile shot, then pitched forward!

From off to the right came the barking of six-shooters. Abruptly, above the roaring reports, sounded the thudding of heavy hoofs, as the cows, frightened into action by the shooting, rose from their beds and started off in a wild stampede! The maddened animals were running straight toward the two nighthawks, coming in to join their partners. A horse screamed as it stumbled, then went down in the rush. Frantically the steers rushed on, straight for the camp. No power on earth could stop that wild dash!

Jeff tried to turn his pony. The little beast swung faithfully around, then suddenly went to its knees, the sudden halt flinging Jeff over its head. A shot from the campfire had downed Jeff's mount.

For a brief moment, Jeff lay helpless, stunned by the fall. Behind him he could hear the rapid approach of the running cattle, the very earth thudding from the shock of hundreds of pounding hoofs. Then, as Jeff's head cleared a trifle, he saw Frank Randall approaching him at a run from the other side of the fire!

Jeff thought his last moment on earth had arrived. Randall was closing in fast, coming close for a certain, finishing shot. Jeff struggled frantically to one elbow, raised his six-shooter and pulled trigger.

The hammer fell on an empty shell. Jeff's gun cylinder was empty!

CHAPTER 16

For a brief moment Jeff thought his gun had merely missed fire. Randall was closing in on him rapidly now.

"Damn you!" Randall snarled. "I'll shoot that bandanna off'n yore face and see who you are!"

He stopped a scant few yards from Jeff, jerked the stock of his rifle to shoulder and fired! But Jeff had thrown his body to one side. In his excitement, Randall's shot missed. Again Jeff raised his six-shooter and again the hammer fell with a deadening click. Jeff realised then that his gun was empty.

Randall was just steadying himself for a second shot, when Jeff raised his arm and flung his useless weapon with all the strength at his command. Straight through the air flew the heavy forty-five, striking Randall full in the face, even as he pulled trigger on another shot!

The rifle bullet whined viciously off into the night as Jeff leaped from the earth and jumped for Randall. His first blow took Randall on the shoulder. The man staggered back, recovered, and again lifted his rifle muzzle to bear on Jeff. The next instant Jeff was on him, fighting like an insane tiger, shooting in heavy, punishing punches to face and body.

In the heat of the fight they had forgotten the stampeding cattle. Even as Randall dropped to his knees under Jeff's onslaught, the noise of the thundering hoofs struck the cowboy's ears.

Instinctively Jeff yelled to Randall: "Look out, cowpoke! Those cows are—"

The words were never finished as Jeff sprung back several feet, moving as swiftly as he knew how.

The panting, sweaty form of a steer, momentarily insane with fright, swept past Jeff just as he jumped backward. In the confusion of the moment, Jeff saw the huge charging body of the steer strike Randall's shoulder and spin him off balance. A second red, plunging body knocked Randall to the earth before he could recover. Then the man's struggling form was blotted from sight as the moving herd crushed it to earth amid the choking clouds of dust.

For an instant Jeff closed his eyes against the scene. When he again opened them, there was nothing to be seen of Randall except a strangely flattened form, half submerged in dust. Jeff gulped and looked after the departing cows, thundering off across the range with no slackening of speed, then he turned again to seek Three-Star and Hefty.

A moment later Jeff's heart leaped with relief as the moonlight showed him two riders trotting through the dust clouds. Apparently his two partners were uninjured.

"Hi! Cowboys!" Jeff yelled.

"You all right, Jeff?" Hefty's voice cut through the night. Three-Star was at his side voicing similar words.

"All right, boys," Jeff replied quickly. The two punchers quickly reached his side. Jeff went on, "Things certainly started to pop from the minute we arrived, didn't they?"

"Sure did!" Hefty nodded.

"What become of those two nighthawks?" Jeff asked.

"We headed to meet 'em," Three-Star said. "They chose to fight it out. They was throwin' down on us as we neared the herd. We wa'nt holdin' back our fire neither. 'Bout that time those steers went spooky and rolled their tails. Me'n Hefty saw 'em start and got out of the way. But those nighthawks didn't move fast enough, they was so busy rollin' lead at us. The herd hit 'em like a tornado, and they went down in the rush. We don't know if we finished 'em or if it was the steers, though we shore had a hand in it."

Jeff quickly explained what had happened, then the three went to look for the bodies of Barker's other punchers. Three of them had been caught in the rush of stampeding cattle and crushed to death. Their features bore little resemblance to those of human beings, though Hefty and Three-Star identified them as Pat Lagou, Squint Morrell and Frank Randall. Two more men whom Jeff or his companions had dropped, near the fire when the fight first opened, were identified as Chuck Hastings and Crooked-Nose Simpson.

Jeff and his companions were silent for a long minute. Finally Hefty said, "Looks like Barker will have to hire a few more hands. His crew has been whittled down some."

Jeff frowned. "Dammit, I hate to feel responsible for these deaths. Howsomever, they opened the firing. Barker and his gang have been doing their best to get me. They're trying to steal the Rocking-D. Gosh, I can't just sit still and let 'em get away with ideas of that kind."

"Don't you let it worry you, waddy," Three-Star advised quietly. "Judge Colt is the only law for you to follow, until this business is cleared up and you can get a square deal from the law in town. I'm figurin' Barker is responsible for yore paw's death, and I'm cravin' to pin it on him proper. What we handed out tonight, and what happened, is no more'n just. . . . Well, Jeff, had we better be slopin' after those cows?"

"Let 'em run," Jeff said. "They're headed in the direction we'd be drivin' 'em anyway and makin' better time than they would for us. Let 'em run. Things seem to be comin' our way a mite. . . . At that we better not hang around here too long.

Barker or some of his gang might show up. Let's drift."

Jeff looked for and found his gun not far from the body of his dead pony. Stripping off saddle and bridle and saddle-blanket, he placed them on one of the Rocking-D mounts picketed a short distance from the camp.

Once mounted, it wasn't long before Jeff and his companions overtook the steers. The herd had slowed down considerably by this time and were ready to settle down again for the night, but Jeff and the other two kept them on the move now.

As soon as the cows appeared to be thoroughly quieted, Jeff reined his pony close to Three-Star's side, saying, "You and Hefty can keep this stock movin' without me now. We're leavin' plenty 'sign' for Barker to follow, so I don't want any hitch in makin' delivery of this stuff to Madero. I'll ride ahead and let him know we're comin'. In case he's not at the Border line, I'll have to ride south a few miles and locate him—"

"Know how to find his hideout?" Three-Star asked.

Jeff nodded. "Yes, I had full instructions from him. Thought I might need the information someday. I'll be lookin' for you, through Cayuga Canyon, about dawn. You can slow up a mite, once you strike Cayuga. Once in that canyon we could stand off Barker and his gang for a long time, if we had to. You know, just in case he should discover this job, right away, and follow us up. . . . S'long."

"S'long," Three-Star echoed.

Jeff swung his mount over to the opposite side of the shuffling herd and informed Hefty as to his plans, repeating the things he had told Three-Star.

Hefty nodded. "All right, we'll be lookin' for you after we get through Cayuga Canyon."

"You got it. *Adios*!"

"S'long."

Jeff jabbed spurs to his pony's ribs, the little beast broke into a swift, ground-covering lope and in a few moments Jeff was lost to sight in the night as he moved up, far ahead of the herd.

Drifting clouds obscured the moon now and then. For the rest of the night the two cowboys kept the steers moving along as fast as possible. The cattle were strung out in a long line by this time, Hefty riding on one side, Three-Star on the other.

The moon was low on the horizon and the two cowboys were herding their charges into the foothills of the eastward sweep of the Trozar Range, when, suddenly, from up ahead and off to one side a bit, Three-Star caught sounds that denoted the presence of other cattle.

Three-Star called out a few words to Hefty relative to "keepin' these cows movin'" and spurred forward to investigate. He had just drawn abreast of the leaders of his own herd, when an involuntary gasp of surprise opened his mouth and for a moment he checked pace, trying to decide what to do.

The shadowy figure of a masked man in red had left the smaller herd and was riding to meet Three-Star. The masked man said abruptly, without any preliminary greeting, "Here's about fifty Herefords I've been picking up the past few days, Three-Star. They're Rocking-D stock. Throw 'em in with that herd you're drivin' and take 'em along."

"Say—say, what the hell!" Three-Star exclaimed. "What's the idea, Jeff?"

"Jeff my eye!" The Red Rider chuckled. "Guess again, hombre." The masked man had pulled to a halt and was now turning his horse away from Three-Star. "Don't ask questions. Just take these cows and keep a-goin'."

In the swiftly fading light of the moon, Three-Star tried to solve the Red Rider's identity. That he was dressed in a red suit of some kind, with a long coat of the same color descending from his shoulders, was about all the cowboy could ascertain. And with a red mask, of course. "Dang it," Three-Star growled, "if you ain't Jeff Deming, I'll eat my aunt's old tabby cat for breakfast! Who in time are you, anyhow?"

The Red Rider's horse was moving away now as its rider spoke pleasantly over one shoulder, "Curiosity has been known to kill a cat. Well, if you insist on knowin' who I am, I'll tell you that I'm—the Red Rider of Smoky Range. Don't forget to take these Herefords away with you." The Red Rider was fading into the darkness now, moving fast.

"Hey, Jeff, wait a minute," Three-Star yelled. "I want to talk to you."

The only reply was an amused laugh that floated back on the early morning breeze. The moon was completely gone by this time.

"Well, may I be everlastingly hung for a thievin' sheep-herder!" Three-Star howled his exasperation, snatching off his hat and dashing it to the earth. Then, cursing himself for losing his temper, he leaned down from the saddle to pick it up.

By this time the steers herded by Hefty had passed on ahead in the darkness. Hearing the sounds of Three-Star's angry exclamations, Hefty left his charges and came riding up.

"What's wrong, cowpunch," Hefty asked as he approached Three-Star, "did somethin' go wrong, or did you lose somethin'—"

"No, we found fifty more cows—"

Hefty exploded, "Where in the name of the seven bald-faced buzzards did these cows come from—?"

"Jeff—the Red Rider—Jeff—" Three-Star gasped weakly. "Fact is, Hefty, I don't know what to say—"

"What you talkin' about? I kinda thought I heard voices over this way once."

"You did—the Red Rider—Jeff—"

"Hey, quit tellin' riddles. What happened?"

Gathering his thoughts, Three-Star finally managed to relate in a relatively calm voice just what had taken place. Before he had concluded, he was interrupted.

"The Red Rider!" Hefty yelled. "And you say it was Jeff—with a red mask on his face and dressed in red—"

Three-Star shook his head in perplexity. "Dam'd if I know what to think now. At first I was certain shore it was Jeff—just about his build. Now I don't know. But who else would be pickin' up Rocking-D stock and turnin' it over to us? On the other hand, why should Jeff run a whizzer like this on us?"

"Don't seem like Jeff would," Hefty said thoughtfully. "Could it have been Madero? He's in on this scheme and is danged friendly to Jeff—"

"By gosh, it might have been Madero at that—" Three-Star hesitated suddenly, then, "Still, I don't know. He didn't talk like Madero. This hombre made *habla* in cow country language—"

"Aw shucks," Hefty broke in, "ain't you ever heard Otón Madero talk straight English?"

"English?"

"Well, American, then. He can talk as good

American as Lucita does. That accent of his is just put on for effect like. He knows people expect it, and Madero always was plumb accommodatin'."

Three-Star's voice sounded hopeless, "Well, it's got me beat."

"We'll both be beat," Hefty remembered suddenly, "if we don't take this gatherin' of cow critters and turn 'em in with our cows. Hope them beasts ain't stopped movin'. They was kinda showin' signs of wantin' to bed down when I left 'em. C'mon, rattle yore spurs. We got to get movin'. We'll settle this with Jeff when we meet him—"

"Dammit!" Three-Star growled, "I already asked him if he was Jeff and he give me the laugh. 'Course, mebbe it really wa'n't him."

"We'll ask him again," Hefty said. "He can't do no more than shoot you for askin' and I hope he does. You said somethin' about curiosity exterminatin' felines. Mebbe it'll kill a bow-laigged cow nurse too! C'mon, let's get these cows movin'."

With the assistance of their two smart little cow-ponies, Hefty and Three-Star quickly got the Red Rider's donation of fifty Herefords strung out and moving at a fast trot toward the first herd of cows. In time the smaller bunch caught up and merged with the larger which had commenced to show an inclination to stop. But the two cowboys kept the steers on the move.

The sun was lifting above the lowest peaks

of the Arribas Mountains when the cows were herded through Cayuga Canyon and out into the open country that was Mexico. Jeff and Otón Madero, with a crew of mounted *vaqueros*, were waiting at the southern end of the canyon when the two cowboys arrived with their charges.

Madero spoke quick orders to his men who took charge of the herd, then followed Jeff to meet Hefty and Three-Star.

"Nice work, fellows," Jeff complimented, smiling, as the four horses and riders came together. "You made good time too." He ran his gaze swiftly along the line of cows filing past to the accompaniment of clouds of dust and shouting *vaqueros*, then frowned. "Say, I reckon I made a mistake. I told Señor Madero we'd have about one-hundred-fifty steers to deliver." Running a quick, practiced eye over the cattle, he nodded, then, "Yep, there must be about two hundred there, anyway. Now how could I make a miscount of that kind?"

Three-Star finished lighting a cigarette, inhaled deeply, and asked, "Say, Jeff, what did you do with yore pretty red suit and that red mask?" He winked broadly as though there were some secret between them. Jeff looked puzzled, then smiled as Hefty broke in, "Yep, Jeff, poor ol' Three-Star has gone clean batty. He's runnin' off at the head again. Jeff, he thinks yore the Red Rider."

"Me?"

"Uh-huh."

Here Three-Star broke in to tell what had happened and how they had gained the extra fifty cows. Hefty put in a word here and there, and finally the tale was finished, though both cowboys suspected that Jeff or Madero—perhaps both—already knew the story.

"*Por Dios*!" Madero exclaimed. "The Red Rider he decided to help Jeff, no?"

"You mean to tell me you ain't him, Señor Madero?" Hefty said warmly.

"*Socorro*! No, Señor Hefty." Madero's eyes twinkled genially.

Jeff laughed shortly. "You boys needn't look to me for the answer, because I just haven't got it. Just the same we'll be passin' a vote of thanks to the scarlet ridin' hombre that donated these extra cows. We can use 'em. And don't worry about the Red Rider so long as he's friendly to us. Eventually, we'll mebbe find out who he is." Jeff looked searchingly at Madero but received only a nod and a bland smile.

Madero finally said, "Whoever he is, he is fighting agains' Quinn Barker. That should be enough for you boys."

Jeff nodded. "Just the way I look at it." He turned to Three-Star and Hefty, "You two better slope for Gunsmoke City now. If you push hard you can make town before there are many people up. Don't enter town by the main street. Come in the back way. The owner of the Blue Front Livery sleeps late and never locks his doors. You can come in by the rear way, put your horses up, and then slip up into his hayloft and get some sleep. He'll never know the difference. He sleeps like a log. In case you should be suspected of this rustlin', he'll swear to an alibi for you. So far as he knows you'll have been there all night. I'll keep in touch with you through Señor Madero, and let you know when there's another bunch of stock to be lifted. . . . Get driftin', now."

CHAPTER 17

It wasn't long before Quinn Barker commenced to realise that he had, in the parlance of the range, bitten off more than he could chew in his crooked plans to gain control of the Rocking-D outfit.

While he had no proof, he came to the conclusion, and rightly, that Jeff had been responsible for the "running off" of the cattle.

The missing cattle had been trailed through Cayuga Canyon to the Border line; farther than that, Barker and his men didn't dare go. Pike Collier, who had automatically shouldered the duties of Ike Eaton, was out daily in search of the rustlers, but could learn nothing except that the stock had been taken into Mexico.

Jeff hadn't stopped with that first job. Time after time, he and his friends ran off small bunches of unguarded Rocking-D cattle, striking always when Barker least suspected such a move. And, usually, the Red Rider showed up somewhere along the trail with an additional number of cows which were being herded along by Jeff's friends. Strange to say, the Red Rider's participations in the rustling always happened when Jeff was supposedly riding ahead of the herd to warn Madero of its arrival. This, if nothing else, strengthened in the minds of Hefty and Three-Star the firm belief that Jeff Deming was, in reality, the Red Rider.

As his cows disappeared with monotonous regularity, Quinn Barker grew angrier and angrier.

In desperation, he finally decided upon a plan to place guards at the entrance to Cayuga Canyon on the American side, and thus capture, and kill, if possible, the rustlers. Gabe Torango, Scar Tonto, Bulldog Higgins and Herb Rivers composed the guard. The four were heavily armed and ready for fight.

For five nights they waited, hidden in the brush, at the entrance to the canyon, but no cattle were driven through. Toward dawn of the fifth night, the four men grew restless and rose to stretch and yawn. It was that darkest period of the night, when the moon is gone and the first gray streaks of daylight have not yet appeared.

"Hell's bells!" Torango grumbled. "Them rustlin' hombres must know we're here, waitin' for 'em, and got scairt out. Let's slope back and tell Quinn we're just wastin' time."

Scar Tonto stretched his arms wearily. "Suits me. I'm gettin' plumb tired of sittin', cramped up, in that brush every night. Let's get slopin'."

Similar remarks were voiced by the other men. Horses were finally led out of the brush, cinches tightened. The men rolled cigarettes, lighted them. For a few moments they stood smoking, then climbed into saddles.

"Seems like," Herb Rivers suggested, "we ought to wait until daylight, anyway. Can't tell what may happen come dawn."

The four riders sat, saddles close together, arguing the question. Abruptly, not far distant, a horseman took form in the gloom. Torango saw him first and warned the others. The horses were backed away a trifle. Hands went to gun-butts.

"Who are you?" Torango demanded in a loud voice. "Give us a hail, mister, or we're—"

"Shut yore loud mouth, Gabe," came the instant reply in gruff tones. "That voice of yores can be heard clear to Gunsmoke, I reckon. It's me, Barker, of course. See anythin' tonight—?"

"Aw, it's only Quinn," Herb Rivers commented. The four men at once relaxed, removing hands from gun-butts, without stopping to question the matter. The rider commenced to take more definite form in the gloom, though they couldn't make out his features. It was still too dark for that.

"We were just gettin' ready to leave, Quinn," Torango was saying. "We been here five nights now and ain't seen a thing—" He halted abruptly.

"You see something now, don't you," the supposed Barker was saying crisply, in a changed voice. "Up with 'em, you hombres! Quick! Stick 'em up!"

By this time the speaker was close enough for the four men to see that they were confronted by the Red Rider. In either hand the man in the crimson mask gripped a Colt forty-five!

With a howl of rage, Gabe Torango reached for his gun. A burst of fire exploded from the Red Rider's right hand. His left hand moved . . . smoke and flame roared through the night. One slug entered Torango's shoulder; the other broke the gun-arm of Herb Rivers, who had also experienced a streak of rash recklessness along with Torango.

The hands of Bulldog Higgins and Scar Tonto were high in the air by this time.

"When I say 'put 'em up' I mean it," the Red Rider snapped. "Higgins, you and Tonto unbuckle yore belts and drop 'em on the ground. Move fast. My trigger finger is shore itchy."

The two men quickly complied with the command.

The Red Rider continued, "Now get over there to Torango and Rivers, and keep 'em from fallin' off their horses. Then roll your tails out of here— plenty pronto!"

Torango and Rivers were still in the saddle, filling the night with mingled curses and anguished groans.

"Get goin', you cheap excuses for badmen," the man in red said contemptuously, "and tell Quinn Barker we don't want to see any more of his jackals hangin' around this canyon. Next time he sends a bunch of you *malo* hombres to watch Cayuga Canyon, you all better be prepared for trouble in big batches. I'm losin' patience. I've given you a warnin'. If you don't take it, it's your own funeral. Slope, pronto, now!"

In a silence broken only by the amused chuckles of the Red Rider and the groaning of Torango and Rivers the four men started off through the darkness for the Rocking-D.

Two miles farther on the quartet drew rein to complete some much needed bandaging with bandannas on Rivers and Torango.

"Say, do you know somethin'," Tonto growled as he tightened a knot, "that Red Rider's voice sounded like it might be Jeff Deming's—"

"I ain't so shore of that," Bulldog Higgins grunted. "Me, I sort of had Chape Stock in mind."

"Yo're crazy, Bulldog," Tonto snapped. "Anyway, regardless who we think it is, we'll pretend it sounded like young Deming. We'll tell Quinn that—"

"Quinn will shore be fit to be tied when he hears the news," Torango groaned through the pain of his wounded shoulder. "I can see him frothin' at the mouth right now. Suppose you—ouch!— suppose we do say it was Deming, what then?"

"Get Barker to offer a reward for Deming's capture," Tonto explained. "That'll put a heap of folks on his trail. He'll get caught and—"

"And I bet that'll stop the rustlin' too," Higgins nodded, catching the idea. "It's a right move, Scar."

"I think so myself," Tonto said virtuously. "This stealin' of our stock has got to be stopped."

"*Our* stock!" Higgins grinned through the graying light. "That's a good one!"

CHAPTER 18

No doubt about it, it was a reckless, fool-hardy thing to do. Jeff, himself, even in his most rash moments, admitted that much. But caution was thrown to the winds when he reached the point where he felt it was absolutely necessary to see and talk with Lucita. Swash-buckling indiscretion was ever the natural heritage of young love.

The sun was blazing down with fierce intensity one mid-morning, when Jeff pulled rein on the trail that led into town. He'd been pushing his pony hard; the horse needed a short rest before continuing. Jeff hooked one knee over the saddle-horn, while the pony shuffled slowly through the dust, and rolled and lighted a brown-paper cigarette. He fanned his lungs deeply with the smoke and exhaled slowly as he drew from an inner pocket a folded "Wanted" bill which Hefty had sent him by Madero.

A slow smile spread over Jeff's face as he unfolded and again examined the reward bill. "Hm," he muttered, "One thousand dollars reward for the capture, dead or alive, of Jeff Deming, alias The Red Rider. . . . Well, I'll be danged! I wonder if Pike Collier congratulated himself on bein' a good guesser when he had these bills printed. . . . And I'm wanted for murder, robbery and rustlin'."

Jeff refolded the paper and put it away. "Dang it all," he mused, "I should be insulted. If my hide isn't worth more than a thousand dollars to Barker—but mebbe the state is offerin' this reward. Collier would fix that part. I'll betcha Barker's money is runnin' low. His profits this year are shore to be whittled down a heap—and there's plenty Rocking-D cows too."

Jeff chuckled to himself, "It certainly makes me feel sad to think of Quinn Barker losin' money, while I've been pilin' it up on the sale of Rocking-D cows. Barker will be gettin' plumb desperate, one of these days, and doing something rash, or I miss my guess."

A short time later Jeff loped boldly into Gunsmoke City. The day was unusually hot and at this hour most people were remaining indoors. Straight to Lucita's little shop Jeff rode. Here he pulled to a halt and slipped from the saddle. Tossing his pony's reins over the tie-rail, Jeff strode boldly to the door, which stood open, and entered the cool, dim interior with its blanket-hung walls.

Lucita was alone, arranging the silver and turquoise jewelry in the glass case to the left of the entrance. Her face lifted as he stepped into the shop and dropped the bandanna that stretched across his nose.

For a moment all of the color left the girl's face, then it flowed back. "Jeff!" she exclaimed, mingled joy and concern in the one word.

"Yeah, it's me, honey," he grinned ungrammatically. "Gosh, I just had to see you. Couldn't stay away a minute longer."

The girl hurried around the glass case, hands outstretched. Jeff took her hands in his, drew her close. There ensued a few minutes of silence before Lucita stepped back. Then her words came with a rush, fear tinging the tones, "Oh, Jeff, people are saying you're the Red Rider— that you're a rustler. Pike Collier is boasting that he'll shoot you on sight. Father was in yesterday. He tells me everything is all right, but—"

"I'm rustlin' some," Jeff admitted grimly, "if you can call it that. Haven't touched anything that I haven't a right to, though. Yes, I know about that reward bill. So—Collier is goin' to shoot me on sight, eh? I got a good notion to go find him—"

"Jeff!" There was a wail in the girl's voice, her eyes were wide. "You mustn't! I want you to leave right this minute and ride straight out of town without stopping to see anyone. Will you do it?"

Jeff nodded, somewhat reluctantly. "Gosh, that makes it look like runnin' away, but I'll do it. I'll do anythin' you say, girl. Lucita, you know I couldn't refuse you anythin'—by gosh! I nearly forgot—just a second—"

Without completing the words he reached into his pocket, then quickly took one of the girl's slim brown fingers and slipped something on it. The next instant Lucita was gazing down on the diamond ring that blazed on her hand.

"Jeff! It's beautiful. I—I—"

"Rode to the capital three days back to get it," Jeff beamed happily. "Now I feel like I really had some hold on you. I just got back before dawn this mornin'. I come straight here, after talkin' to your dad at the Cayuga Canyon camp. I told him how things stood between us, but I reckon he's been doing some thinking on his own part, because he didn't seem very much surprised when he shook hands with me."

"Oh, Jeff . . ."

Another long silence took place, the heads and bodies of the two close together.

Neither Jeff nor the girl noticed the face of a man at one of the shop windows. The fellow flattened his nose against the pane for a few moments, then turned hastily away and hurried off, down the street.

Ten minutes drifted quickly past before Jeff prepared to take his departure. "I'll slip in again, one of these days," he said. "I'll have to see you more than ever now."

"You're to ride straight out of town, remember," the girl admonished him, "just as fast as your horse will carry you."

"I remember," Jeff grinned, donning his sombrero. "I'll do just as you say. Nothin' else," he promised. "*Adios*, honey."

"*Adios*, Jeff."

The young puncher stepped out of the shop, drawing the door closed behind him, and started toward his horse. As he stepped into the blinding white light of the sun, the thundering report of a Colt gun caused him to jerk abruptly around. At the same instant, a leaden slug splintered the tie-rail!

There, coming at a run, were Pike Collier and Bulldog Higgins, guns in hands. Collier was just lifting his gun for a second shot. Gray smoke drifted on the breeze. Jeff's hands darted to holsters. A swift, double streak of light flashed along the barrels as his guns came out of their scabbards. A savage jet of white fire burst from his right hand, then his left!

Gunfire roared along the street. Somewhere a man yelled. Running footsteps cleared a space in Jeff's vicinity. Bullets were kicking up dust spurts all around Jeff now. A slug ripped through the bandanna that lay at his throat.

Jeff swayed to one side, thumbed another shot. Pike Collier had halted and gone into a crouch near a store entrance. Now he unfolded suddenly, spun twice around, and crashed to the plank sidewalk.

Higgins was closing in fast, his guns flaming.

Again Jeff released a leaden slug. Higgins stopped, his body stiffening. He tried to get into motion again, took three stumbling steps. One shoulder struck the dust as he suddenly sprawled out in the roadway.

But Higgins wasn't done yet: cursing, the man braced himself on one hand. From the other hand came sharp lances of smoke and fire. Jeff felt something like molten steel burn along one thigh. He laughed grimly. In his right hand a gun kicked, exploded. Higgins snarled something unintelligible, then suddenly coughed and sagged forward on his face!

CHAPTER 19

Drifting powder smoke slid away on the hot breeze. Jeff cast a quick glance at Higgins and Collier, who both lay in queer unnatural positions. Neither moved. Jeff realized they were dead. For a moment he felt a bit sick. He didn't like this killing.

A scream sounded in Jeff's ears. His mind reverting to Lucita, Jeff swung quickly around to see the girl's form framed in the open doorway of her shop. Her face was ashen white. Her lips moved in excited speech, but Jeff failed to catch the import of her words. His gaze followed her pointing arm.

There, coming along the street at breakneck speed, was Quinn Barker, quirting his horse like a madman. Behind him rode some twenty other hard-bitten individuals, recent hirelings of the Rocking-D: plug-uglies, cattle thieves and badmen—every one of them.

Leaping over the tie-rail, Jeff caught the reins of his frantic pony, vaulted into the saddle without touching the stirrup. The horse reared, pivoted on hind hoofs as Jeff swung it around. Already Barker and his followers were commencing to unleash their lead, the bullets buzzing like angry bees as they winged past or knocked up tiny spurts of dust in the roadway.

"Ride, Jeff, ride!" Lucita screamed.

Jeff drove in his spurs and the little pony came down to all fours, then darted ahead, rapidly lengthening its stride. Almost immediately Jeff commenced to draw away from Barker and his followers.

A few vagrant shots still flew around and behind him, but Jeff was quickly drawing away from his pursuers, who were holding their fire now. He examined the wound in his leg. Higgins's bullet had just grazed the skin of his left thigh. The wound wasn't serious and had already stopped bleeding. Jeff urged his horse to greater speed, raising a trifle in the stirrups to ease his weight, his head crouched closely to the horse's neck.

The chase continued as the roadway left the town and spread out across open range. The Barker gang was about three hundred yards to the rear now, riding silently in grim pursuit.

It had been Jeff's first intention to reach Cayuga Canyon where he had figured to find Madero and the *vaqueros*. Then he had remembered: Madero and his men were to break camp that morning. They wouldn't be there. Besides, Jeff's horse was commencing to tire, and although it hadn't slackened speed, Jeff could hear the labored breathing of the wiry little beast. Its withers were foam-flecked; its hide streaked with dust and sweat. The horses of the Barker faction had been fresh when the chase started.

At the edge of the foothills of the Trozar Mountains was an old abandoned building which had once, in days long past, served as a combination trading post and fortress. Now it was crumbling and weather-beaten, the sole reminder of the days when Smoky Range had figured as the scene of countless battles with the Apaches.

It was toward this old building that Jeff was heading. If he could only reach it, he felt he'd be relatively secure.

Years before, when Jeff was first learning to ride a horse and his brother Bob had reached the age when he could ride alone, their father had taken the boys to the old building and shown them a trap-door in the floor. Beneath this trap-door was a long, underground passage that led into the hills at the rear of the place, before opening to the surface. John Deming himself had helped to build that tunnel, and Jeff remembered, now, how he had thrilled at his father's story which related how John Deming and other men had once, after a three-day fight, made their escape from marauding Apaches by this underground route.

Jeff was within a half-mile of the ancient building when he felt the pony stumble. At the same instant there sounded from behind the sharp crack of a Winchester. The pony had been hit, but immediately recovered and labored on. From

Barker and his men came wild yells of delight:

"That's the stuff!"

"Good shootin'!"

"Bring down the horse!"

"Capture him alive!" Barker's voice bawled above the din.

The firing increased!

Jeff's pony struggled bravely on, responding to its rider's urging, and for a few minutes actually commenced to draw away from the pursuing horde. The old adobe building was only five hundred yards distant now. He could see the weather-beaten door standing partly open. The distance to his goal lessened to three hundred yards . . . two hundred . . . one hundred fifty. . . .

The pony staggered suddenly, regained its stride and staggered again. This time it could scarcely keep going. Wild yells of triumph sounded at Jeff's rear, drawing closer and closer every instant. Jeff heard a sickening thud as a bullet smashed into the pony's hide. Then another and another.

Abruptly the little horse went to its knees. Expecting this calamity, Jeff had already loosened his feet from stirrups. As the horse crashed quivering to the dusty earth, the cowboy leaped from the saddle and started a swift sprint toward the half-open door of the building.

The place loomed larger as he drew near. Only a few more yards now to shelter. His mind worked swiftly as he sped over the hard, sun-baked earth. He'd bar the door, then make for the underground passage. A new thought came to him: suppose the bar was no longer there. Well, he'd shut the door anyway and . . .

There came the staccato drumming of running hoofs closing in. Jeff heard the swift *swish* of lariats sailing through the air. He tried to duck, twisted swiftly around, but the movement came too late. The hempen loops dropped about his body, tightened, and jerked him savagely from his feet at the very door of the old fortress.

"Nice work, boys!" Barker shouted triumphantly to the two ropers who had accomplished the capture. "I reckon you'll collect that reward!"

Jeff struggled to his feet, threw off the ropes and leaped for the entrance to the building, but the maneuver was useless now. Even as he gained the threshold, Barker closed in, jabbed a six-shooter against his spine!

"Better hold it, Deming," Barker snarled. "I'll be pluggin' you on damn little excuse!"

Jeff realized he was trapped. There seemed to be no way out of the difficulty. Reluctantly he raised his hands in the air. The next moment, Scar Tonto stepped forward and jerked the guns from Jeff's holsters.

"Figurin' to stand us off in this old buildin', eh?" Barker rasped in Jeff's ear. "Well, if yo're so anxious to get inside, I'll help you out."

Raising his fist, Barker struck Jeff brutally on the side of the head.

Had the cowboy been facing the badman, he might have evaded the blow by ducking, or at least rolling his head with the force of the impact, but as it was, he didn't even know the blow was coming. The force of rage behind Barker's fist sent Jeff staggering across the big room where he ended with a crash against one wall and dropped to the floor.

Instantly he was up, righteous anger overcoming cold reason. He sprang forward, fists swinging. Before he could reach Barker, Scar Tonto and another man leaped in, shoving their guns against Jeff's middle,

"Slow down, Deming," Tonto laughed nastily, "or you'll be a dead hombre in another second—"

"Let him come, let him come," Barker yelled eagerly. "I got his finish in this smoke-rod of mine. I'll take the fight out of him!"

The sight of Barker waiting there, gun gripped in fist, bloodshot eyes blazing with the desire to kill, suddenly sobered Jeff. He cooled down, laughed scornfully. Without his guns he wouldn't have a ghost of a chance. He backed away from the guns in the hands of Barker's henchmen. By this time the rest of the gang had swarmed into the room.

"I reckon I know when I'm stopped, Barker," Jeff said coolly. "You'll notice I said 'stopped,' not 'licked.' This game isn't ended yet by a long shot; when it is you'll be where you belong—either in jail or surrounded by six silver handles. And I'm bettin' it's a wooden overcoat, if I have anythin' to say."

"You won't have," Barker growled savagely. "Yore finish is due to arrive plumb sudden. I'll teach you to rustle my cows and parade around in a red suit—"

"Not to mention the shootin' of Higgins and Collier," Tonto snarled. "Plain murder that's what that was—"

"Self-defence," Jeff corrected. "Higgins and Collier started that shootin'. As for rustlin' cows, I have as much right to 'em as Barker has—"

"How you figurin' that?" Barker roared wrathfully.

Jeff said coldly: "Barker, you haven't any rights to the Rocking-D and you know it. You forged that bill of sale. Barker, you're a murderin' skunk and you'll hang for killin' my father!"

Barker choked. His features flushed angrily. Two or three of his men had laughed at Jeff's words. The name he had called Barker had bitten deeply. For a moment he couldn't speak, then, "Skunk, am I? I'll show you. By God, this is yore finish. It's a good idea to let you shoot it out with two men. We'll see just how fast you are." Barker's lips spread in a nasty grin, exposing tobacco-stained teeth that resembled more nearly the snarl of some maddened beast. "Shore, we'll give you yore guns, Deming—and you'll be facin' me and Tonto! Now, are you game?"

Jeff didn't answer at once. He was sparring for time. Three-Star and Hefty must have been in Gunsmoke City. Surely they would have heard what had happened and arrive with help before long.

Barker rasped, "You aimin' to take all night to think it over? Looks like *yore* yellow streak is commencin' to show, Deming."

Jeff said, level-voiced, "Night is a long time away yet, Barker. Nope, I won't require all night, nor the rest of the day, either—"

"Well, decide plumb pronto!" Tonto spat out.

"How in time can a fellow decide anythin'," Jeff stalled, "with you murderin' coyotes standin' around. My life happens to be mighty important to me. I've got to give this thing careful consideration. Give me a little time alone, Barker."

Barker started to refuse, then nodded grudgingly.

"We'll give you half an hour—alone," Barker consented. "Here, in this buildin'. At the end of that time, you'll either face me and Scar Tonto, or we'll hold a necktie party with you on the end of the rope."

Jeff's heart leaped. A half-hour—alone. The laugh would be on Barker. Inside of half an hour, by using the underground passage, Jeff could be far, far away and hidden among the foothills. Then Jeff's spirits dropped at Barker's next words:

"Yeah, we'll leave you alone," Barker was saying, "but we won't take any chances of you puttin' up a battle when yore time is up. Yore hands and feet will be tied. It'd be just like you to rush us the minute we come in here, and we'd have to shoot you to keep you from escapin'. We got our minds set on this duel now, and we want things to run off smooth. . . . Boys, get some piggin' strings and hawgtie this hombre—tight!"

CHAPTER 20

Five minutes later Jeff was alone, bound hand and foot, arms behind his back. He was seated on the floor of the old building, one shoulder resting against a side wall. The door was closed. From outside came the voices of Barker and his crew. Jeff's eyes strayed around the big empty room, resting a moment on the narrow oblong loopholes in the thick adobe walls, then his gaze moved on to a far corner where he knew the trap-door was situated, cunningly set flush with the plank flooring where it wouldn't readily be noticed. The planking in the room was covered with rubbish of one kind and another—a couple of tin cans, old newspapers, a bit of broken harness—and thickly carpeted with the dust of years, though this dust was now some-what scuffed from the feet of the room's recent visitors.

The length of oaken timber standing in one corner, near the door, caught Jeff's eye. This was intended to be employed to bar the door from the inside. Jeff noticed the iron brackets at either side of the door jamb in which the bar was supposed to rest. The brackets were rusted and cobwebby, but looked as though they would still stand a great deal of forcing before they gave way.

Dang it! There must be some method to get out of this fix. Jeff thought, If I could only get that door barred, then I'd have time to work on these rawhide thongs. Mebbe the ragged edge of one of those old tin cans could be used for cutting. But how can I . . . ? Jeff tugged and strained at his bonds, but they held firmly, the rawhide strips cutting into his wrists with each effort.

Finally Jeff gave it up. There was nothing left for him but to face Barker and Tonto. In the face of such uneven odds it looked like the end. True, Jeff had outshot Higgins and Collier, but that was different. As gunmen the two were greatly inferior to Barker and Tonto. Also, Collier and Higgins had been firing while they were running toward Jeff, thus rendering their marksmanship the more inaccurate. Of the two men Jeff was about to face, Scar Tonto was the more dangerous, each of his Colt weapons bearing ominous notches cut into the walnut butt.

The door was pushed suddenly open. "Time's up," Barker announced shortly. "Deming, if you got any prayers to say, you better get busy. . . . And don't be expectin' any of yore friends here to save you. When we cut off the trail to come here, I left a man hid in the brush to see if anybody followed us from town. My man just arrived with the news that he saw a gang of riders headin' off toward Cayuga Canyon. Don't know just who they were. My man wasn't close enough to tell. But he kind of thought he recognized old Chape Stock at the head of the group. 'Nother feller looked like that Three-Star hombre." Barker grinned nastily. "You wa'n't expectin' to meet any of yore friends at Cayuga Canyon, were you?"

"Cut out the talk, Barker," Jeff interrupted coldly. "I'm not hankerin' to hear you spill any of your conversation."

"Sooner have us spill lead, eh?" Tonto sneered.

Jeff stared coldly at the man until Tonto averted his eyes. Now with all hope of help from his friends gone, Jeff suddenly decided he might as well get the fight over with as soon as possible. His face was pale, but composed; his nerves steady.

"Cut them strings, boys," Barker ordered harshly, "and give Deming his guns. It appears like he's anxious to be croaked." The rawhide thongs were quickly removed and Jeff climbed stiffly to his feet. He felt his guns being thrust into holsters.

"A couple of you fellers keep him covered, until we're ready," Barker commanded. "If Deming tries to pull before we give the word, drill him plenty prompt."

Arrangements were quickly made. Jeff took his stand against one side wall of the room. Standing some distance apart, backs to the opposite wall, were Scar Tonto and Barker. Tonto was near the front of the building, not far from the open doorway. Barker was stationed in the far corner, only two or three yards from the hidden trap-door. The two men stood so far apart that Jeff saw at once it would be extremely difficult to watch both at the same time. Tonto carried two guns in his holsters; Barker but one. Jeff planned to down Tonto first and take a chance of Barker missing with the first shot he fired.

One of Barker's men suddenly started for the doorway. "Me, I'm gettin' nervous about flyin' lead," he announced in a shaky voice. "Reckon I'll feel better outside."

"Me, too," came another voice, and a second man rushed for the outside.

The idea took quick hold upon the others. There ensued an abrupt dash for the doorway. In a minute no one remained in the room, except Jeff and his two opponents.

Barker's face clouded up like a thunderstorm. "Come back here, you yeller rats!" he ordered angrily.

No one made a move to obey. The men were rapidly edging back from the open doorway. Barker waited a moment, then snarled peevishly, "All right, you worms. Stay out! But one of you has got to give the signal to start this duel. Nobody can't say this fight won't be run square and proper. You, Henderson!" Barker spoke to an ugly-browed individual, in dirty overalls, standing just outside the door. "You come in here and give the signal. If you don't I'll drill you proper when we get finished with Deming."

"Aw, hell, chief—" Henderson protested.

"Come in here!" Barker roared.

Henderson gulped, then reluctantly slouched back into the room. "What'll I do, chief?" he asked in shaky tones.

"Get over in that corner, near Deming," Barker growled. "You won't get hit there. Count for us; one—two—three. Like that. On the word *three* we go for our shootin'-irons and commence throwin' lead. . . . Deming, is that clear to you!"

Jeff nodded coolly. "*Three* is the signal that announces Old Man Sudden Death for you and Tonto. Do *you* understand, Barker? Then, let's get goin'."

Barker chuckled evilly. "Just a minute, Deming. We forgot to tell you before, but we only left *one* ca'tridge in each of yore guns!"

Jeff laughed scornfully. "You goin' to talk all day and all night too? I'm not kickin'. Two ca'tridges are all I need for two sidewinders. Wait'll you feel 'em rippin' in—"

Tonto swore at Jeff impatiently, then said to Barker, "C'mon, Quinn, let's get this business finished."

Barker glared at his partner, then at Jeff. Jeff said, "Barker, Tonto's right. We want to get this

225

business finished. What are you stallin' for? Lost yore nerve?"

A flush of hot rage swept Barker's features. He quickly went into a half-crouch, finger-tips hovering close to holster.

"Henderson," he grated savagely, "you can start countin'!"

CHAPTER 21

A tense silence had descended on the room, broken only by the breathing of the four occupants. A few faces peered around the sides of the doorway, but for the most part Barker's crew was staying well back out of danger of possible stray bullets. Jeff glanced quickly at Barker, then settled his gaze on Scar Tonto's crouching form. In that moment it came to Jeff that Tonto resembled a rattler, coiled to strike.

Henderson gulped, opened his mouth to start counting, but no sound issued forth. The strain of waiting was commencing to tell on Barker. "Dammit, Henderson!" Barker snarled, "how many times have I got to tell you to start countin'?"

Henderson cleared his throat, shifted his weight uneasily, then spoke: "One!"

Jeff's elbows crooked ever so slightly. His fingers were tingling to grip gun-butts. He wondered just which chambers of his cylinders held the two cartridges. He'd have to keep thumbing hammers until the cylinders revolved to the proper positions.

"Two!"

Henderson again shifted weight, preparatory to speaking the third count. His gun arm moved involuntarily, and at the movement, the peering eyes at the doorway were suddenly jerked back out of sight. Henderson knew he was overdue on the third count. He'd better give it.

At that instant, before Henderson could speak the final word, there came an abrupt interruption:

The hidden trap-door in the corner suddenly flew back, and the upper half of a man's body, attired in red, emerged swiftly into view! In either hand the masked man held a Colt gun!

"Reckon it's about time I took a hand in this," the Red Rider snapped, leaping lightly into the room. Before anyone could make a move to prevent it, he had jabbed his right-hand gun muzzle against Quinn Barker's ribs, even as Barker had turned to see whence had come the strange voice. The Red Rider's other gun was covering Tonto and Henderson.

For an instant everyone appeared to be hypnotized by the Red Rider's sudden appearance. Then Barker found his voice, "Wha—what—who—?" he commenced to stammer.

"Tell your men to get away from that entrance," the Red Rider snapped. "Quick, or I'm borin' you, Barker! . . . Jeff, I'll keep these hombres covered. Bar the door. Hurry!"

Even as Jeff hurried across the floor, he plucked cartridges from belt, flipped back the gate of one of his forty-fives and finished loading the cylinder.

At the doorway he had a brief glimpse of curious, hate-twisted features. A couple of the gang made as though to reach for weapons, but sight of the gun in Jeff's hand put an end to that thought.

"I'll be borin' the first hombre that comes near one of these loopholes," Jeff snapped, as he slammed the door in their faces and dropped the oaken bar into place.

A howl of baffled rage arose on the other side of the barred door.

"Henderson," Jeff ordered, "you get over there by Barker and Tonto. Things are coming my way for a spell."

Quinn Barker and Tonto stood like statues, stricken dumb with amazement at the sudden turn of events, as Henderson shuffled across the floor and took his place at the other wall. The eyes of the three were riveted upon the Red Rider who was clothed in a suit of red corduroys, riding boots, and a crimson cloak of some light material that hung from his shoulders. Across the upper half of his face was a red cloth mask through the holes of which could be seen a pair of stern, piercing, gray eyes. A Mexican sombrero of red felt topped the dark hair.

"It's three against two," the Red Rider was saying tersely. "Barker, I've heard everything that passed since you came here. I've been listening in that underground passage. Didn't know that existed, did you? I've been here, living here, on and off, and you never dreamed of it. Before you start in to steal the Smoky Range blind, you should learn yore range, hombre. . . . You want a duel, eh? Well, Jeff and I will try to accommodate you. Jeff, load your guns."

"I'm ready to roll lead right now," Jeff said eagerly. His heart was pumping like mad. Who was the Red Rider? That voice sounded so familiar.

"Who—who are you?" Barker stammered, white with fear and an unknown terror that clutched his craven heart.

The Red Rider laughed softly. "I reckon I might as well let you know before I kill you, Barker. . . . You dirty coyote, I'm the man that trusted you, the man you tried to steal from—and you succeeded to a certain extent. I'm the man you ordered murdered. I'm—hell, Barker, *now* do you know who I am?"

As the words were finished, the speaker holstered one gun, raised his hand and swept the mask from his features. Barker emitted one startled cry of terror.

The Red Rider was the true owner of the Rocking-D, *John Deming!*

"Dad!" Jeff yelled.

Barker staggered back as though he had seen a ghost. His face was livid with fear. His body trembled like a leaf in a gale. "You—you—" he gasped hoarsely, shrinking against the wall. "It's a lie! It can't be! Yo're dead, Deming. I—I—I saw your dead body! No, no—this is a trap of some kind. I—I—Deming, give me a chance. I didn't mean—I—you—"

Barker choked, one hand tore frantically at his throat as he babbled unintelligible nothings. He crouched against the wall, cringing in a horror-stricken awe of the incomprehensible. That this man whom he had thought dead should suddenly arise from the grave to confront him was too much for Barker's quivering nerves. The man was in a state of near collapse from the shock and surprise John Deming had given him.

"Pull yoreself together, Quinn," Scar Tonto yelled suddenly. "We ain't beat yet!"

Taking advantage of the situation, Tonto raised his guns. Jeff's right hand jerked to one side . . . belched lead and flame! Tonto pitched to the floor, convulsive muscular action working his triggers and sending shot after shot roaring harmlessly across the room.

Tonto's words had snapped Barker back to reality. With the desperation of a cornered rat, he leaped wide of the wall, his gun barking savagely. His first shot missed. John Deming's hand flicked up. The Red Rider's guns spoke twice as Barker fired. Barker halted in midstride, stiffened. Then his knees bent, he twisted limply to one side and crashed down!

Jeff had whirled from finishing Tonto, to face Henderson who was just getting into action. The swift explosions of the young cowboy's gun rocked the building. Henderson was knocked back against the wall as though hurled there by some gigantic, invisible force. For a brief moment he remained erect, eyes starting from their sockets, jaw hanging open in stunned amazement. Quite suddenly he wilted and slid to the plank flooring.

Jeff turned just as Barker went down. John Deming stood back, guns ready. Powder smoke drifted in the room. Barker struggled to rise, then a shudder ran through his body. For a moment his booted feet drummed spasmodically on the floor, then he was still. John Deming relaxed. Jeff darted forward, stooped over Barker's body. An instant later he rose with the forged bill of sale and the deed to the Rocking-D and handed them to his father.

John Deming glanced at the papers, crumpled the spurious bill of sale into one pocket. The deed he handed back to Jeff, saying somewhat awkwardly, "Keep it, son. By rights it should be yours." He didn't meet Jeff's gaze for a moment, then he said slowly, "I reckon that's all, boy. We licked 'em."

Jeff said gravely after a moment, "They're all finished, Dad. Yes, we licked 'em—you and I."

Their hands met, closed in a firm clasp. The elder Deming's eyes were wet. "Lord, son," he faltered, "I wasn't sure if you'd—"

A sudden pounding on the door interrupted the words. Momentarily Jeff and his father had forgotten there were fifteen or eighteen of Barker's gang outside. A voice yelled, "What's doin' in there? Let us in, Barker!"

John Deming raised his voice. "Barker's done for," he called. "So's Tonto and Henderson. You coyotes better clear out of the Smoky Range country."

From outside came the confusion of many excited voices, as the full meaning of Deming's words fell on the men's ears. Low growls swelled in their throats as they commenced to realise they wouldn't get the money promised by Barker. Then they remembered the reward bill which offered money for the apprehension of the Red Rider.

One fellow in a sudden fit of temper lifted his gun and emptied it against the front wall of the building. That started things: the next instant a fusillade of bullets struck the adobe structure, or whined viciously through the loopholes. Luckily neither Jeff nor his father was hit.

"You fellers better come out," yelled an angry voice near the door. "We're figurin' to collect that reward. If you come out you won't be harmed. We'll turn you over to the law authorities. But suit yoreselves. That reward reads 'dead or alive.' What's it goin' to be?"

"Think we dare trust 'em?" Jeff said.

John Deming shook his head. "They wouldn't take a chance on losing us. Pro'bly fill us full of lead first chance they got. We don't dare step out there—especially after us killin' Barker and Tonto and Henderson. They'd want to avenge the death of their friends. If they had time to cool down, they might listen to reason, but in their present state—"

"About the way I figure it," Jeff broke in quickly. "C'mon, we'll slip through that trap-door and make a getaway through the tunnel. We can hide in the brush until they leave. I got a heap of questions to ask you, but I can wait a few minutes—"

"No use, Jeff," John Deming shook his head. "Too late to escape by the tunnel. I was back in the hills when I first saw you ridin' here, and I made a bee-line for the passage. Left my horse at the other entrance. Most of those coyotes saw me emerge at this end, so they'll be lookin' for the way in, and watchin' it. With my horse standin' there, it'll be easy to locate—"

"Well," came an ugly interruption from the other side of the door, "what's yore answer? Are you surrenderin'?"

Jeff left his father's side and went to one of the front loopholes. He couldn't see the door from that position, but thrusting his gun through the opening he fired at random. That his guess was good was attested by the yelp of pain that followed the shot.

"There's our answer!" Jeff yelled, ducking back.

The words were greeted by a torrent of cursing and another hail of lead spattered against the building.

"You'll pay for that, Deming," came a new voice. "You needn't think you can stand us off long. Some of our shots is shore to land where they'll do the most good. And you can't escape, neither. We discovered where that underground passage comes out—"

"Why don't you try gettin' us that way, then," Jeff laughed scornfully. "We'll be waitin' for you—"

A rifle bullet whined savagely through one of the narrow loopholes, ricocheted around the room, glanced off a far wall and thudded into the floor near Scar Tonto's dead body.

Jeff quickly reloaded his empty cylinder chambers. "Throw a shot through one of the loopholes, Dad," he exclaimed. "We'll stand 'em off as long as our lead holds out."

"After that, what?" John Deming asked grimly.

Jeff laughed recklessly. "We'll think about that time when it comes, Dad. I don't know of anybody I'd sooner make a last stand with than you."

Jeff darted quickly to the bodies of the dead men, ripped off their belts to secure additional ammunition. Barker's belt was half full; his gun cylinder held three unexploded cartridges. Tonto's loops yielded a scant fifteen loads; the chambers of his forty-fives gave up four more. Henderson's cartridges proved to be useless, as he had carried a forty-four six-shooter, a calibre not adapted for use in the guns of Jeff and his father.

A moment later the two men were dashing from loophole to loophole, their hands spitting lance-like streaks of white fire. With a roar of rage, the men on the outside brought their guns into action. For a few moments the din of firing was terrific!

CHAPTER 22

It was Trigger Texas who was responsible," John Deming was saying, twenty minutes later, between shots from a side wall loophole.

By this time the gang had scattered for the shelter of the brush that dotted the outskirts of the building. Every loophole in the building was covered now, and from their places of concealment the members of the Barker faction were sending in a slow steady fire that found the openings and sent leaden messengers of death winging through the big room. In this way the outlaws held the advantage: it was the custom of Jeff and his father to dash to a loophole and empty their guns blindly in the hope of finding a mark. Occasionally a yelp of pain would attest their success in this method, but more often the lead was wasted, as they didn't dare show themselves sufficiently long to locate their targets. The outlaws, well hidden among the mesquite and other growths, could well afford to bide their time and conserve ammunition.

"I was on my way to the Rocking-D, carrying the satchel with the twenty-five thousand Barker had paid me. His note for the balance was with the money," John Deming was explaining to Jeff, who was listening from across the room. "I'd just got to the top of Crooked Pass when Trigger Texas held me up, took my gun away and threw it over the pass—"

"Did you recognize Texas in the dark?"

Deming nodded. "Recognized his voice. It shore made me feel bitter to think of his disloyalty. But I wasn't afraid; never dreamed that he intended to kill me. He herded me up the slope to that old shack where you and yore friends had been stayin'. He was holdin' his gun on me all the time. When we got to the shack he made me place a blanket over the window so no light could show out, in case anybody came over the Pass. 'Course, nobody was li'ble to, rainin' like it was—"

"I did," Jeff said. "That cabin was dark when I passed. Pro'bly that blanket—"

"I heard, afterward, that you had trailed me that night, son. Anyway, at the time, I thought I was just about the only hombre that would risk his neck on that trail in bad weather. I've learned a heap of things since then—"

John Deming jerked back suddenly as a leaden slug *ping-ng-g-ged* past his head to bury itself in the opposite wall. Instantly Deming sent a shot flying toward the spot in the brush where the flash of gunfire had appeared. He shifted position to another loophole and went on:

"You know how greedy Texas always was. That night he stuck me up he was worse than ever. He'd got the money I'd been carryin', but he wasn't satisfied with that. His clothing was pretty ragged, so he ordered me to strip and give him mine. The dirty coyote even made me give up that old gold ring I'd worn since—"

A shower of adobe dust flew into Jeff's face as a bullet struck the corner of a loophole he was approaching. Instantly he returned the fire and was rewarded by hearing the thrashing of a heavy body in the brush, though he couldn't catch sight of the man he had hit. He darted across the room and took up a stand close to another opening. "Go on, Dad, sorry to interrupt."

The room was filled with powder smoke now. It hung in low clouds drifting half-way to the flat ceiling, and stinging eyes and throat and nostrils. The day was scorching hot and the room like the inside of a furnace. The air was stifling. There was no water to be had. Jeff's tongue was parched and he knew his father's was in the same condition. In a few moments the elder Deming resumed the account of what had happened.

"As fast as Texas put my clothes on, he stuffed his own in the stove that was in the cabin. You'll remember it was right chilly that night and Texas had started a fire while he waited for the time when I was due along the Pass. He'd been drinkin' while he waited and was plumb talkative by the time he got me undressed in that shanty. He was so sure that I was goin' to die that night that he didn't hold back nothin'—told me of Barker's plan to steal the Rocking-D. Spilled the whole story—didn't hold back a single detail. I could see murder in his eyes while he talked. I stalled along as well as I could, undressin' slow and questionin' him. He was in a boastin' mood and he told me he intended to double-cross Barker, keep the twenty-five thousand and get out of the country. Incidentally, Barker got that money by brand-blottin' my stock and sellin' it on the sly. He'd been stealin' cattle almost since the day I hired him."

"Did he say anythin' about brother Bob?" Jeff asked.

Deming's words came hard for a moment. He said, low-voiced, "You were right about that, Jeff. The rumors you told me about turned out to be facts. Your brother had got evidence that Barker was stealin' our stock, rebrandin' the cows with a Wagon-Wheel, and selling them in the next county. Bob had caught Barker red-handed, but Barker had got away on his horse and headed for town. When Bob reached town, lookin' for Barker, Barker's hired gunman was there, waitin' to embroil Bob in a fight. Barker came into the Red Tiger Saloon, behind Bob, and shot yore brother in the back. Later, Barker, as you know, got rid of all the evidence—"

The elder Deming broke off. For a few moments he couldn't go on. Finally he admitted awkwardly, "It was listenin' to Texas talk that night that made me realize I hadn't given you a square deal when you warned me against Barker. I was pretty much of a skunk in my treatment of you, son—"

"Aw, hell, Dad," Jeff protested, "forget it. We'll—by Cripes! I got him!" Jeff said suddenly, thumbing a swift shot through a loophole. A volley of flaming lead swept into the room and for a minute the two Demings were forced to crouch closely to the floor while the flying slugs whined overhead. A few moments later they were doing their best to return the fire. The rattle of firearms swelled to a mad roar of crashing explosions, then gradually diminished to a desultory firing again. John Deming was swearing softly to himself.

"You hit, Dad?" Jeff queried anxiously, turning a sweat and powder grimed face toward his father.

"Lost a mite of skin off'n the back of one hand," Deming grumbled. "It don't amount to nothin' but it stings like all get out. I'll get on with my story before I get rubbed out, I reckon. . . . All the time Texas was gettin' into my clothing, I was watchin' for a chance to spoil his game. But he kept his gun close to hand, and as I was on the far side of the room I didn't dare try anythin' reckless—"

"Naturally, you wouldn't with that dirty skunk."

Deming nodded. "You can see the fix I was in. I reckon Texas must have felt I was li'ble to make a fight for my life, 'cause he didn't wait to put on his ca'tridge belt before startin' to leave. He backed toward the door, holdin' the satchel of money and ca'tridge belt in one hand, and his gun in the other. It's my guess that he figured to pull the trigger on me, just as he stepped outside."

Deming paused to fill his brier pipe, lighted it, puffed meditatively a few moments and continued, "Texas had just threw open the door and was backing away from me, raising his gun. I'll never forget the look in his killer's eyes. Well, as he was backin' toward the doorway, he bumped against a chair and sort of stumbled. That was my chance and I took it without losin' any time. I jumped across the room and grabbed him. He fired twice while I was comin', but missed both times. As I closed with him he dropped his ca'tridge belt and the satchel of money, but hung on to the gun which same we were both fightin' for by this time. Finally, I was lucky enough to bend his wrist around, just as he pulled trigger on his third shot. Instead of hittin' me, that bullet ploughed into Trigger Texas's body—"

"Damn' if this isn't just like a story," Jeff broke in admiringly.

"It's a story I don't want to go through again," John Deming said grimly. "Up until the moment when Texas's shot entered his own dirty carcass,

242

I was never so near death in my life. The minute Texas was shot, he dropped his gun and staggered outside. I grabbed up the weapon and followed him, figurin' to finish the job. The rain was comin' down in torrents by that time. Just as I left the shack, I heard the rocks startin' to roll on the slope, up above me. The noise got nearer and nearer and louder and louder, until it sounded like an express train roarin' down on me—"

"The landslide!" Jeff exclaimed.

"Yo're right, boy. I knew at once it was a landslide and I lost my interest in finishin' Texas off. But I did want that money. I turned and ducked back into the shack, grabbed the satchel and the ca'tridge belt Texas had dropped on top of it, and run for my life!"

"But, Texas—" Jeff commenced excitedly.

"I'm gettin' to that, son. When I left that cabin, lucky I run in the right direction. I got out of the cabin just in time. Dimly in the dark I could see Texas staggerin' around. I yelled at him, but it was too late. He was headin' toward Crooked Pass, directly in the path of those tons and tons of movin' rock as they came thunderin' down the slope. I heard splinterin' wood, and there went the cabin I'd been in only an instant before—"

John Deming suddenly broke into a fit of righteous profanity as a flying slug picked the brier pipe out of his mouth and sent the bits of wood hurtling in all directions.

"Dammit!" Deming growled. "That was the sweetest pipe I ever owned too!"

He emptied his cylinders and started to reload while he talked. "To cut a long story short, that avalanche was over before I'd realized what had happened. The whole slope was swept clean as a whistle and Texas, my horse, and the house had been carried over the pass and into the ravine below. Boy, much as I hated Texas, it made me feel sort of sick all over. I knew nothin' living would have a chance for life in that landslide. Luckily, Texas had left his horse picketed farther over, where he had been waitin' for me on the Pass. The landslide had missed Texas's horse so I had something to ride—"

The shooting swelled to a shrill crescendo as bullets commenced to whine through the room. The besiegers were growing impatient at the opposition with which they were meeting. Jeff and his father fired and reloaded, fired and reloaded. Their guns grew hot to the touch. What was more important, their ammunition was running low.

The firing of the enemy guns slackened after a time. At Jeff's urging John Deming went on with his story.

"It's kind of funny to think of now," he smiled grimly, "but when it was all over I was part way to town before I realized I didn't have on a stitch of clothin', except my suit of red underwear and my socks. Texas had stripped me pretty clean. But, boy, I was too excited to get cold. I was doin' a heap of thinkin', let me tell you. I never dreamed that body would be found. I figured Texas would be buried under rock—"

"It was Trigger Texas we buried—"

"It was Trigger Texas you buried," Deming nodded. He went on, "I didn't know exactly what to do at first, but figurin' that Texas's body would be buried under that avalanche, I thought I'd lie low for a spell until I saw what happened. You see, son," Deming explained awkwardly, "I was feelin' like pretty much of a fool, after the warnin' you gave me against Barker and the way I'd treated you. I was plumb ashamed of myself and I felt lower than a buzzard. A man hates to admit he's wrong. I didn't want to face anybody for a spell—least of all my own son that I'd treated so rotten."

"Aw, shucks, Dad, I wish you wouldn't talk that way."

Whup! A bullet crossed the room, thudded into the opposite wall. Jeff snapped two quick shots in reply.

"Anyway," John Deming continued, "I thought I'd keep out of sight and let you handle the reins. I figured you deserved that much of a chance, anyway. And remember, I was too ashamed to face you right away. But there was one important thing to do, and that was to get that bill of sale

I'd given Barker. I knew he planned to stay at the hotel that night—he'd mentioned where his room was—so I rode into Gunsmoke City and entered Barker's room. He'd been drinkin', plenty, I reckon. The room smelled plumb alcoholic. I see he was pretty bleary-eyed; he didn't even get a good look at me. I got the bill of sale and lighted out, headed for the Border."

Jeff had been watching the top of a sombrero as it slowly appeared at a loophole across the room. One man, bolder than the others, was being boosted up by a companion. He paid for his rashness with his life. As his face came into view, Jeff slipped one quick shot toward the loophole. The face abruptly disappeared!

After a few minutes John Deming resumed, "Just below the Mexican line there's an old Mexican living. He's a pretty decent sort, is old Pablo Nunez. I knew I could trust him to keep a secret. I went to Pablo's place and he got me some clothes. Later, I returned to Gunsmoke City one night and learned that everybody was talkin' about a mysterious Red Rider—"

"But how did you learn that?"

Deming smiled. "Well, I sneaked into town and listened under windows here and there. That give me an idea. I wanted to devil Barker before I had a showdown with him. I went back to Pablo's place and told him the sort of clothes I wanted. You see, Barker had just caught a glimpse of my red underwear that night. I decided to carry out the idea. Pablo went to one of these Mexican shops where they carry fancy suits and so on—and the Red Rider was started on his career. Pablo has helped a lot. He used to come to Gunsmoke and listen to gossip. Between us, we kept pretty much in touch with what was going on."

"That first time you held up the sheriff's office—" Jeff commenced.

"I wanted to get yore gun that they was holdin' against you for evidence," Deming explained. "So they wouldn't suspect any friend of yours being back of it, I grabbed all the guns in sight. Boy, I've been in and out of town, I don't know how many times, listenin' under folks' windows. I've scouted around the range. Went to spy on the Barker crowd at the ranch on a couple of occasions."

"You sure enjoyed yourself," Jeff chuckled.

Deming laughed softly. "I shore did. You see, I'd been a hard-headed old fool, but now I was comin' to my senses. I commenced to enjoy bein' reckless, what with stickin' up sheriffs, scarin' off badmen, helpin' you rustle cows, and helpin' you escape from jail."

"Was that you slipped my gun into my cell and got my horse?"

John Deming nodded. "I trailed you that night you left the jail. I was close by when you ran into Madero on the road out of town. I overheard your plans for turnin' rustler. I never dreamed to be proud of a son of mine turnin' rustler, but I was that night. It showed fightin' spirit. After that, I was never very far away from you. Our build and voices bein' alike, it's not surprisin' you were suspected of bein' the Red Rider."

Jeff exclaimed, "Gosh, to think of you bein' alive and lookin' after my welfare all the time—"

"Except when they tried to lynch you, son. I didn't know about that until later. If it hadn't been for your friends—especially the Maderos—and say, Jeff, you forget anythin' I ever said about Lucita and her father. From now on you and me will be runnin' the Rocking-D—provided we ever get out of here alive. It don't look like we will. That gang out there has been quiet quite a spell now. They must be cookin' up somethin'."

At that instant there came a sudden rush of feet across the earth at the front of the building. Something heavy thudded against the door! Again came the crash! The oaken door shuddered under the impact. It looked like the end.

CHAPTER 23

Jeff and his father rushed to openings on either side of the door, but were driven back by the hail of bullets that poured through the loopholes.

"They've got one of those old timbers that were piled outside," Jeff cried. "Usin' it for a batterin' ram!"

Deming nodded grimly. "That's the plan, boy. It looks like the finish. How's yore ca'tridges holdin' out?"

Jeff ran quick fingers along his belt loops. "Only four in my belt," he exclaimed in dismay. "Three in one gun, two in the other."

"Give me those four in yore belt, boy," Deming said quickly. "Mine's plumb gone. We'll give those coyotes a hot reception when they bust in. Make every shot count."

A third time the battering ram smashed against the door. The supports that held the bar in place were torn loose. The bar thudded to the floor. The door was swinging open! Crash! Another blow.

"Hold your fire until they come in!" Jeff shouted.

The next instant the door was flung to one side, but the outlaws were scattering back now. Jeff and his father were working their guns like madmen. It was all a crimson blur of sweat and smoke and thundering guns. A man toppled across the threshold.

Suddenly Jeff discovered that his hammers were falling on empty shells! John Deming's gun was already empty. He raised it in his hand, hurled it at the nearest invader, who had already turned to flee.

From outside came the swift thudding of horses' hoofs . . . wild cowboy yells . . . a renewed crashing of forty-fives. The attackers were scattering wildly in all directions. The roaring of Colt guns suddenly ceased as cries for mercy ascended on the air.

Jeff leaped over the sprawled figure in the doorway and landed on the earth outside. A yell of pure joy was torn from his throat at the scene that greeted his astonished eyes. There, accompanied by a grim-faced crew of cow-punchers, were Hefty, Three-Star, Chape Stock and Madero.

There were but few of the Barker gang left on their feet by this time and these few were holding their arms high in the air. The others were sprawled in various attitudes on the earth. The atmosphere was thick with powder smoke.

For a time all was in confusion. "It was Lucita that brought us word that Barker and his coyotes were ridin' after you," Three-Star was yelling to make himself understood above the clamor of excited voices. "Hefty and me had been sleepin' late in the livery hayloft. Never heard the shots. By the time we got to the street, later, there was Lucita lookin' for us. She said you'd killed Collier and Higgins. About that time, Madero came ridin' into town. A minute later we ran into Chape Stock. The four of us rounded up all the fightin' hombres we could find in a hurry and lit out on Barker's trail—"

"We pounded leather to Cayuga Canyon first," Hefty took up the story. "Madero told us you knew he'd broken camp, but we thought you might have headed for his hideout on the Mexican side. Anyway, you weren't there. We'd been so shore of findin' you there that we hadn't watched the trail close for sign. We started to head back to town, thinkin' you might have circled wide and come back. On the way to Gunsmoke, Lucita allowed as how she thought she heard gunfire over this way—"

"Lucita with you?" Jeff yelled excitedly, looking around. For the moment he had forgotten his father, hadn't noticed that John Deming hadn't emerged from the old building yet.

"Lucita was with us," Chape Stock put in. "Well, we listened and heard shots too. We headed for here pronto. A mile or so back, Señor Madero wouldn't let the girl come any farther, for fear she'd be hurt when we got here and started fightin'—"

"It wasn't much of a fight," Three-Star again,

"but we closed in and gave what was needed. We rounded up the whole crew of snakes, except what yore responsible for. Say, what were you doin' in—"

"And something else," Hefty interrupted, "we been talkin' to Otón Madero. He ain't a bandit a-tall, but a Spanish naturalized citizen of these United States. Can you beat that? He's been working for the Government Secret Service—"

"—been trailin' Barker for years," Three-Star said excitedly. "Under another name he's been wanted for a mail robbery up Utah way. That happened before he come to Smoky Range. It was only recent that he got clues pointin' to Barker as bein' the man—"

Hefty broke in, "Madero figured if he could get Torango to talk he'd learn somethin' definite. Barker stayed in town last night. Early this mornin', Madero went to the Rocking-D. Torango and Rivers were there, nursin' wounds they claim was given 'em by the Red Rider. Torango and Barker had quarreled about that, Barker claimin' that Torango should have captured the Red Rider. Torango was sore and spilled everythin' he knew about Barker—"

"Whoa, whoa!" Jeff cut in, laughing. "You're both talkin' like you had to say everythin' at once." He nodded toward the old adobe building, adding, "Barker's dead in there. Tonto, too—"

252

"That's great," Three-Star commenced. "I was wonderin'—"

"Anyway," Hefty rushed on, "we'll have Torango and Rivers where they can be picked up. They won't leave the Rocking-D—"

"And Madero's got a bit cattle outfit over in Mexico," Three-Star cut in. "That's how he could take all those cattle off'n our hands. And—and—and—"

Jeff glanced at Madero, who had been sitting his horse, listening gravely to the excited conversations. The Spaniard's eyes twinkled. Jeff grinned. "Shucks! Lucita told me all that this mornin', when I was in Gunsmoke. Why don't you waddies get some up-to-date news. Wait until I tell you something, where's—?"

Jeff broke off, looking beyond the men and horses toward open country. Nearly half a mile away he spotted Lucita approaching on her pony. Jeff waved wildly, then, reaching up, seized Three-Star by the belt and jerked the astonished cowpuncher out of the saddle. He paused only long enough to gesture toward the doorway of the adobe building before vaulting to the back of Three-Star's horse.

"Take the hoss with my blessin', old son," Three-Star grinned. Abruptly the grin vanished from his face as he glanced toward the building. His jaw dropped. "What the devil!"

John Deming had just emerged from the

doorway. Unable to resist the temptation to fool his friends a little longer, he had again donned his red mask before stepping into the open air. Astonished exclamations rose from Chape Stock, Madero and the others as the Red Rider approached with long strides.

Jeff was already getting into motion, as he laughed over one shoulder, "There's your Red Rider, cowpokes. Remember there's a reward on his head—but try to collect it. I got pressin' business with Lucita!"

He swung the pony away from the open-mouthed group of riders, who sat staring at the mysterious man in red, and spurred to a swift lope to join Lucita. . . .

The girl's eyes were brimming with happiness as the two drew close together. The horses stopped, stood quietly, shoulder to hip. Jeff reached over, gathered the girl in his arms.

Eventually Lucita drew her head to one side, glancing over Jeff's shoulder toward the group of men clustered about a tall figure in red clothing. The distance was too great for Lucita to distinguish John Deming's features.

"Jeff!" the girl exclaimed. "The Red Rider—?"

Jeff nodded, grinning widely. "Come on—let's go see him. We'll tell you all about it. He's your prospective paw-in-law. Everythin's cleared up; the story's ended."

Lucita looked quizzically at Jeff, her mind not

254

quite comprehending the words. Then her head dropped back to his shoulder.

"The story's ended?" she murmured. "Cowboy, I think you're wrong. It's just beginning. . . ."

Center Point Large Print
600 Brooks Road / PO Box 1
Thorndike, ME 04986-0001 USA

(207) 568-3717

US & Canada:
1 800 929-9108
www.centerpointlargeprint.com